William Shakespeare, Henry L. Hinton

Shakespeare's Tragedy of Romeo and Juliet

as produced by Edwin Booth

William Shakespeare, Henry L. Hinton

Shakespeare's Tragedy of Romeo and Juliet
as produced by Edwin Booth

ISBN/EAN: 9783337383671

Printed in Europe, USA, Canada, Australia, Japan

Cover: Foto ©Andreas Hilbeck / pixelio.de

More available books at **www.hansebooks.com**

30 cents.   **BOOTH'S SERIES OF ACTING PLAYS.**   No. 5.

SHAKESPEARE'S

TRAGEDY OF

ROMEO AND JULIET

AS PRODUCED BY

EDWIN BOOTH.

Adapted from the Text of the Cambridge Editors, with Introductory Remarks, &c.,

By HENRY L. HINTON.

NEW YORK:

PUBLISHED BY HURD & HOUGHTON,

459 BROOME STREET.

INTRODUCTION.

'WHATEVER is most intoxicating in the odor of a southern spring, languishing in the song of the nightingale, or voluptuous on the first opening of the rose, is breathed into this poem. But, even more rapidly than the earliest blossoms of youth and beauty decay, it hurries on from the first timidly-bold declaration of love and modest return, to the most unlimited passion, to an irrevocable union; then, amidst alternating storms of rapture and despair, to the death of the two lovers, who still appear enviable as their love survives them, and as by their death they have obtained a triumph over every separating power. The sweetest and the bitterest, love and hatred, festivity and dark forebodings, tender embraces and sepul chers, the fullness of life and self-annihilation, are all here brought close to each other; and all these contrasts are so blended in the harmonious and wonderful work into a unity of impression, that the echo which the whole leaves behind in the mind resembles a single but endless sigh.' These are the beautiful sentences in which Schlegel seeks to distill the spirit of our play.

The present adaptation of this drama is merely a slight curtailment of the original; only one unimportant transposition is made. The adaptation which has long held the stage is the one made by Garrick. It contains many additions and presumed improvements, which show, to say the least, very little respect for the original author. But he whose judgment led him to cut out the grave-diggers in *Hamlet*, as a superfluous addition, can easily be imagined capable of introducing an inferior funeral dirge into *Romeo and Juliet*, and of making Romeo live to carry on a lengthy dialogue with Juliet after he had drank the poison, which the apothecary expressly tells him, 'if he had the strength of twenty men,' 'would dispatch him straight.'

After all, perhaps Garrick can not be so severely censured, when, after more than half a century, the great German poet and scholar, Goethe, made such havoc with the text of this play, when he undertook to recast it for the stage. To use the words of his biographer, Lewes, 'Goethe had so little sense of what was dramatic, that he actually opens his version like a comic opera, with a chorus of servants, who are arranging lamps and garlands before Capulet's house. Maskers pass into the house; Romeo and Benvolio enter and *talk*. They tell the audience of the family feud which Shakespeare made us see.'

In Goethe's version Mercutio is quite a new character. He is deprived of much of his original vivacity and gayety; his celebrated Queen Mab speech is entirely cut out. He prefers not to dance at Capulet's masque, for fear that his exquisite shape, which was known to everybody, should betray him. Paris actually makes love to Juliet, instead of formally seeking her hand through her father, and the tragic ending of the piece is simply told as a moral by the Friar.

The original play is too long for an evening representation, and as we are compelled to shorten it, we have endeavored to do so in such a manner as to detract as little as possible from the spirit of the original work.

In following this play with the text in hand, the auditor may observe a slight departure from it in certain instances. The concluding lines of some speeches, in accordance with the custom of the stage, will be broken up, or otherwise changed, to avoid the rhymes with which in the original they are, as it were, wound up, and which, in the delivery, are often found to mar the effect.

It is always a matter of interest to know who were the first to essay important rôles. Richard Burbage, we are told, was the original Romeo. In an elegy upon him in a manuscript of the early part of the seventeenth century, his Romeo is thus spoken of:—

> 'Poor Romeo never more shall tears beget
> For Juliet's love and cruel Capulet.'

The 28th of September, 1750, was a memorable day in London. The Covent Garden and Drury Lane theaters both announced *Romeo and Juliet*. The rivalry was between the two Romeos, Garrick's and Barry's, and the two Juliets, Miss Bellamy's and Mrs. Cibber's. Doran, in his *Annals of the Stage*, has given us an interesting narrative of the two performances.

'At Covent Garden, the public had Romeo, Barry; Mercutio, Macklin; Juliet, Mrs. Cibber. At Drury, Romeo, Garrick; Mercutio, Woodward; Juliet, Miss Bellamy. On the first night Barry spoke a poor prologue, in which it was insinuated that the arrogance and selfishness of Garrick had driven him and Mrs. Cibber from Covent Garden. Garrick, ready to repel assault, answered in a lively, good-natured epilogue, delivered saucily by Mrs. Clive.

It was considered a wonderful circumstance that this play ran for *twelve* nights successively; Garrick played it thirteen, to show that he was not beaten from the field. At that period the Londoners, who were constant play-goers, demanded a frequent change of performance; and the few country folks then in town felt aggrieved that one play should keep the stage during the whole fortnight they were in London. Hence the well-known epigram :—

> " ' Well, what's to-night ?' says angry Ned,
> As up from bed he rouses ;
> ' Romeo again !' he shakes his head ;
> ' A plague on both your houses !' "

Contemporary journals, indeed, affirm that the audiences grew thin toward the end of the fortnight, but this seems doubtful, as Barry's twenty-third representation, in the course of the season, was given expressly on account of the great number of persons who were unable to obtain admission to his twenty-second performance.

There is no doubt that Mrs. Cibber had the handsomer, more silver tongued, and tender lover. She seemed to listen to him in a sort of modest ecstacy, while Miss Bellamy, eager love in her eyes, rapture in her heart, and amorous impatience in every expression, was ready to fling herself into Romeo's arms. In Barry's Romeo the critics laud his harmony of feature, his melting eyes, and his unequaled plaintiveness of voice. In the garden scenes of the second and fourth acts, and in the first part of the scene in the tomb, were Barry's most effective points. Garrick's great scenes were with the Friar and the Apothecary. Miss Bellamy declared that in the scenes with the Friar alone, was Garrick superior to Barry; Macklin swore that Barry excelled his rival in every scene.

The Juliets, too, divided the public judgment. Some were taken by the amorous rapture, the loveliness, and the natural style of Miss Bellamy; others were moved by the grander beauty, the force, and the tragic expression of distress and despair which distinguished Mrs. Cibber. Perhaps, after all, the truest idea of the two Romeos may be gathered from the remark of a lady who did not pretend to be a critic, and who was guided by her feelings. 'Had I been Juliet,' she said, 'to Garrick's Romeo—so ardent and impassioned was he, I should have expected that he would have *come up* to me in the balcony ; but had I been Juliet to Barry's Romeo—so tender, so eloquent, and so seductive was he, I should certainly have *gone down* to him !'

COSTUME.

In costuming a play the first question that naturally arises is, how did the author intend to array his personages. It is well known that in Shakespeare's time the custom of dressing plays according to the fashion of the period which they were intended to represent, had not been introduced ; only such distinctions of dress were adopted as were in vogue in the time of the author. Thus Shakespeare arrays Shylock in a gabardine, although history says that the Venetian Jews of Shylock's time differed in nothing in dress from Christians of the same walk in life. He makes Mercutio speak of Romeo's 'French slop,' a kind of loose breeches, and satirizes those 'fashion-mongers, who stand so much on the new form, that they can not sit at ease on the old bench '—referring to the bolstered breeches worn by the fops of that time. As, therefore, it would be quite absurd at the present day to array the characters of Shakespeare in the costume of his own period, we are left in this matter to the exercise of our own judgment ; and good taste, as well as modern realism, demands that we should aim at historical accuracy of costume, allowing only such modifications as the exigences of the play may imperatively demand.

The events upon which *Romeo and Juliet* is constructed, took place, according to the ancient tradition, in the time of Bartholomew della Scala, 1303. To the fourteenth century, then, an age rich in varied and gorgeous display, we must look for modes suitable for the decoration of the Dramatis Personæ of the present piece.

It is a mistake to suppose that the costume of the fourteenth century may be obtained from the paintings of Giotto, and his contemporaries ; the painters selected from the past or present such modes as best suited the subjects they treated. For a faithful and complete representation of the costume of this period, we must look to other sources. As we have already said, it was rich in variety. We shall therefore content ourselves in the present article with an enumeration of the most marked features.

One of the most prevalent articles of male attire in all Europe at this period, was a garment which was known in France under the name of *cote-hardie*. It was a waistcoat or jacket, that fitted quite tight to the form down to the middle of the thigh. It was made of the richest materials, and was covered with embroidery and buttoned down the front, whilst a girdle confined it over the hips. But the most fantastical part of this dress were the over-sleeves; they were close-fitting as far as the elbows, and then hung down in long white pendants. A cloak of unusually great length was sometimes worn over the *cote-hardie*. It was furnished with a row of buttons on the right shoulder, and the edges were frequently pinked in imitation of leaves or flowers.

Another remarkable peculiarity in the attire of men at this time, was the capuchin, or hood. It enveloped the head and shoulders, and was buttoned close up to the chin. It had a long queue, that hung down the back in a point. Some gallants twisted it up in a fantastical form and carelessly poised it on the top of the head, and sometimes even placed a beaver hat over it.

Hats and caps were also worn in endless varieties. Toward the latter part of the century, a feather is seen for the first time to grace the head-dress of a gentleman. The sword hung from the girdle directly in front ; shoes were worn ridiculously long, and pointed.

In France and Italy the *cote-hardie* sometimes is seen reaching nearly to the knees, and the capuchin has the addition of *epaulieres* or shoulder-pieces, which formed a sort of false sleeve reaching nearly to the elbows, from which were hung appendages embroidered with gold, or long ribbons reaching to the ground.

The dress of the ladies of high degree was no less splendid. Gold and silver glittered on the garments, and precious stones became very costly from the immense demand for them. The most universally worn vestment was also the *cote-hardie*, which, like that of the men, fitted tight to the shape. It was, however, not quite so long, hardly reaching to the middle. The corners were rounded off in front. The skirt was full and very long, trailing on the ground. The sleeves were similar to those worn by the men, except that the tight under-sleeves extended down on the hands. A large cloak or mantle of gold and silver cloth, still more ample than that worn by the men, sometimes completed this very rich attire.

Immense head-dresses of almost every conceivable shape were prevalent throughout the century; but at one time (about the middle of the century) we find the ladies allowing their hair to ornament their heads without the addition of cap, bonnet, or hood. It was then arranged in one large plait, on each side of the face, with flowers or jewels interspersed. Their shoes, like the men's, were very long and pointed.

But one of the most striking features in the fashion of that age, was the emblazonment of almost every article of dress with armorial colors and devices, so that the *tout-ensemble* was often grotesque in the extreme.

SCENERY.

In the forthcoming revival of this play, at Mr. Booth's new theater, the epoch selected as most in harmony with the spirit of the piece, is the early part of the fourteenth century. The costumes adopted in this performance will, therefore, be similar to those we have described in the preceding pages.

Equal attention will, we understand, be given to a faithful representation of the architecture, household furniture, etc., of the age.

Of the architecture of Verona, we have, it is true, no representations contemporary with the supposed period of the play. This lack, however, is supplied in part by the numerous contemporary representations of the public and private buildings of other Italian cities, and in part by the fact that for hundreds of years Verona has undergone no considerable change in external appearance, and that, therefore, engravings of its present architecture only need such modifications as our knowledge of the period, drawn from the sources above indicated, will warrant.

In verification of the statement that the Verona of to-day differs but little from the Verona of the fourteenth century, read these words of Theophile Gautier: 'Verona, whose name can not be pronounced without thinking of Romeo and Juliet, of whom the genius of Shakespeare has made two realities which history willingly accepts, presents itself to the traveler's eye in very picturesque fashion. . . . . . The Capulets and the Montagues might still quarrel, and Tybalt kill Mercutio in the streets of Verona; the scene is unchanged; the tragedy of Shakespeare marvelously exact. In Verona, as in a Spanish city, every house has its balcony, and the silken ladder has only to make its choice. Few cities have better preserved the character of the middle ages. The pointed arches, the trefoiled windows, the open balconies, the pillared houses, the sculptured corners of the streets, the vast hotels with bronze knockers, elaborate gratings and entablatures, crowned with statues and rich architectural details, which the pencil alone can render, carry you back at once to the past, and make you feel astonished at seeing people in modern costume, and soldiers in Austrian uniform. This impression is strongest in the market-place (Piazza delle Erbe), where the houses, painted in fresco by Paolo Albasini, with their projecting balconies, carved ornaments, and massive pillars, revive the most romantic associations.'

In depicting interiors, the scenic artist, Mr. Witham, availing himself of such memorials in writing and on canvas as have been preserved, has been equally studious to present to the eye of the beholder a true copy of the ' still life ' of the times.

DRAMATIS PERSONÆ

Of this adaptation of *Romeo and Juliet* as cast for its first representation at Booth's Theatre, New York, —————.

ESCALUS, prince of Verona........................ ————————
PARIS, a young nobleman, kinsman to the prince........ ——————————
MONTAGUE, ⎱ heads of two houses at variance ⎰........ ——————————
CAPULET, ⎰ with each other.............. ⎱........ ——————————
An old man, of the Capulet family.................... ——————————
ROMEO, son to Montague..................... .... ·———— —— ——
MERCUTIO, kinsman to the prince, and friend to Romeo..... ————————
BENVOLIO, nephew to Montague, and friend to Romeo...... ———————
TYBALT, nephew to Lady Capulet..................... ————————
FRIAR LAWRENCE, a Franciscan...................... ————————
FRIAR JOHN, of the same order...................... ————————
BALTHASAR, servant to Romeo.......................· ————————
PETER, ⎫   ⎧.................. ...———————
SAMPSON, ⎬ servants to Capulet ⎨.................... ————— ——
GREGORY, ⎭   ⎩.................... ————————
ABRAHAM, servant to Montague...................... ————————————
An Apothecary............·———— ——— Page to Paris.............·————————
First Musician..............·——————— First Servant..............·——————
Second Musician............·———— —— Second Servant............·————————
Third Musician............·————— ——

LADY CAPULET, wife to Capulet...................... ——————————
JULIET, daughter to Capulet...........................··———————————
Nurse to Juliet.............................·————————

Kinsfolk of both houses; Maskers, Guards, Watchmen, and Attendants.

SCENE : *Verona : Mantua.*

————————◆•◆•◆►—————————

NOTE. — The asterisks that occasionally appear in the text refer to the glossary

THE TRAGEDY

O F

ROMEO AND JULIET.

ACT I.

SCENE I. *Verona. A public place.*

Enter SAMPSON *and* GREGORY, *of the house of Capulet, with swords and bucklers.*

Sam. Gregory, on my word, we'll not carry coals.*

Gre. No, for then we should be colliers.

Sam. I mean, an we be in choler, we'll draw.

Gre. Ay, while you live, draw your neck out o' the collar.

Sam. I strike quickly, being moved.

Gre. But thou art not quickly moved to strike.

Sam. A dog of the house of Montague moves me.

Gre. To move is to stir, and to be valiant is to stand: therefore, if thou art moved, thou runn'st away.

Sam. A dog of that house shall move me to stand: I will take the wall of any man or maid of Montague's.

Gre. That shows thee a weak slave; for the weakest goes to the wall.

Sam. 'Tis 'true; and therefore women, being the weaker ves-

sels, are ever thrust to the wall : thérefore I will push Montague's
men from the wall.

Gre. The quarrel is between our masters and us their men.

Sam. 'Tis all one, I will show myself a tyrant : when I have
fought with the men, I will be civil with the maids; and 'tis
known I am a pretty piece of flesh.

Gre. 'Tis well thou art not fish; if thou hadst, thou hadst been
poor John.* Draw thy tool; here comes two of the house of
the Montagues.¹

Sam. My naked weapon is out : quarrel; I will back thee.

Gre. How ! turn thy back and run ?

Sam. Fear me not.

Gre. No, marry ; I fear thee !

Sam. Let us take the law of our sides ; let them begin.

Gre. I will frown as I pass by, and let them take it as they
list.

Sam. Nay, as they dare. I will bite my thumb² at them ;
which is a disgrace to them, if they bear it.

Enter ABRAHAM *and* BALTHASAR.

Abr. Do you bite your thumb at us, sir ?

Sam. I do bite my thumb, sir.

Abr. Do you bite your thumb at us, sir ?

Sam. [*Aside to Gre.*] Is the law of our side, if I say ay ?

Gre. No.

Sam. No, sir, I do not bite my thumb at you, sir ; but I bite
my thumb, sir.

Gre. Do you quarrel, sir ?

Abr. Quarrel, sir ! no, sir.

---

¹ It should be observed that the partisans of the Montague family wore a token in
their hats, in order to distinguish them from their enemies, the Capulets. Hence,
throughout this play, they are known at a distance.

² The manner in which this contemptuous action was performed, is thus described by
Cotgrave :—' *Faire la nique :* to mock by nodding or lifting up of the chinne ; or,
more properly, to threaten or defie, by putting the thumb-nail into the mouth, and with
a jerke (from the upper teeth) make it to knacke.'

Sam. But if you do, sir, I am for you : I serve as good a man
as you.

Abr. No better.

Sam. Well, sir.

Gre. [*Aside to Sam.*] Say 'better :' here comes one of my master's kinsmen.

Sam. Yes, better, sir.

Abr. You lie.

Sam. Draw, if you be men. Gregory, remember thy swashing* blow.   [*They fight.*

Enter BENVOLIO.

Ben. Part, fools !   [*Beating down their weapons.*
Put up your swords ; you know not what you do.

Enter TYBALT.

Tyb. What, art thou drawn among these heartless hinds ?
Turn thee, Benvolio, look upon thy death.

Ben. I do but keep the peace : put up thy sword,
Or manage it to part these men with me.

Tyb. What, drawn, and talk of peace ! I hate the word,
As I hate hell, all Montagues, and thee :
Have at thee, coward.   [*They fight.*

Enter several of both houses, who join the fray ; then enter Peace-
Officers.

Officers. Strike ! beat them down ! down with the Capulets !
down with the Montagues !

Enter CAPULET *and* MONTAGUE.

Cap. What noise is this ? Give me my long sword, ho !
My sword, I say ! Old Montague is come,
And flourishes his blade in spite of me.

Mon. Thou villain Capulet !

Enter PRINCE ESCALUS, *with his train.*

Prin. Rebellious subjects, enemies to peace,
Profaners of this neighbour-stained steel,—
Throw your mistemper'd* weapons to the ground,
And hear the sentence of your moved prince.
Three civil brawls, bred of an airy word,
By thee, old Capulet, and Montague,
Have thrice disturb'd the quiet of our streets,
And made Verona's ancient citizens
Cast by their grave beseeming ornaments,
To wield old partisans, in hands as old,
Canker'd with peace, to part your canker'd hate:
If ever you disturb our streets again,
Your lives shall pay the forfeit of the peace.
For this time, all the rest depart away:
You, Capulet, shall go along with me;
And, Montague, come you this afternoon,
To know our farther pleasure in this case,
To old Free-town, our common judgement-place.
Once more, on pain of death, all men depart.
                    [*Exeunt all but Montague and Benvolio.*
Mon. Who set this ancient quarrel new abroach?
Speak, nephew, were you by when it began?
Ben. Here were the servants of your adversary
And yours close fighting ere I did approach:
I drew to part them: in the instant came
The fiery Tybalt, with his sword prepared;
Which, as he breathed defiance to my ears,
He swung about his head, and cut the winds,
Who, nothing hurt withal, hiss'd him in scorn:
While we were interchanging thrusts and blows,
Came more and more, and fought on part and part,
Till the prince came, who parted either part.
Mon. O, where is Romeo? saw you him to-day?
Right glad I am he was not at this fray.

Ben. An hour before the worshipp'd sun
Peer'd* forth the golden window of the east,
A troubled mind drave me to walk abroad;
Where, underneath the grove of sycamore
That westward rooteth from the city's side,
So early walking did I see your son:
Towards him I made; but he was ware of me,
And stole into the covert of the wood:
I, measuring his affections by my own,
Which then most sought where most might not be found,
Being one too many by my weary self,
Pursued my humour, not pursuing his,
And gladly shunn'd who gladly fled from me.
   Mon. Many a morning hath he there been seen,
With tears augmenting the fresh morning's dew,
Adding to clouds more clouds with his deep sighs:
But all so soon as the all-cheering sun
Should in the farthest east begin to draw
The shady curtains from Aurora's bed,
Away from light steals home my heavy son,
And private in his chamber pens himself,
Shuts up his windows, locks fair daylight out
And makes himself an artificial night:
Black and portentous must this humour prove,
Unless good counsel may the cause remove.
   Ben. My noble uncle, do you know the cause?
   Mon. I neither know it nor can learn of him.
   Ben. Have you importuned him by any means?
   Mon. Both by myself and many others friends:
But he, his own affections' counsellor,
Is to himself—I will not say how true—
But to himself so secret and so close,
So far from sounding and discovery,
As is the bud bit with an envious worm,
Ere he can spread his sweet leaves to the air,

Or dedicate his beauty to the sun.
Could we but learn from whence his sorrows grow,
We would as willingly give cure as know.

Ben. See, where he comes : so please you, step aside ;
I'll know his grievance, or be much denied.

Mon. I would thou wert so happy by thy stay,
To hear true shrift.   [*Exit.*

Enter ROMEO.

Ben. Good morrow, cousin.

Rom.   Is the day so young ?

Ben. But new struck nine.

Rom.   Ah me ! sad hours seem long.
Was that my father that went hence so fast ?

Ben. It was.   What sadness lengthens Romeo's hours ?

Rom. Not having that which, having, makes them short.

Ben. In love ?

Rom. Out—

Ben. Of love ?

Rom. Out of her favour, where I am in love.

Ben. Alas, that love, so gentle in his view,
Should be so tyrannous and rough in proof !

Rom. Alas, that love, whose view is muffled still,
Should without eyes see pathways to his will !
Where shall we dine ?   O me !   What fray was here ?
Yet tell me not, for I have heard it all.
Here's much to do with hate, but more with love :
Why, then, O brawling love !   O loving hate !
O any thing, of nothing first create !
O heavy lightness ! serious vanity !
Mis-shapen chaos of well-seeming forms !
Feather of lead, bright smoke, cold fire, sick health !
Still-waking sleep, that is not what it is !
This love feel I, that feel no love in this.
Dost thou not laugh ?

Ben.   No, coz, I rather weep.

Rom. Good heart, at what?

Ben.   At thy good heart's oppression.
Tell me in sadness, who is that you love,

Rom. What, shall I groan and tell thee?

Ben.   Groan? why, no;
But sadly tell me who.

Rom. Bid a sick man in sadness make his will :
Ah, word ill urged to one that is so ill!
In sadness, cousin, I do love a woman.

Ben. I aim'd so near when I supposed you loved.

Rom. A right good mark-man! And she's fair I love.

Ben. A right fair mark, fair coz, is soonest hit.

Rom. Well, in that hit you miss : she'll not be hit
With Cupid's arrow; she hath Dian's wit,
And in strong proof of chastity well arm'd,
From love's weak childish bow she lives unharm'd.
She will not stay the siege of loving terms,
Nor bide the encounter of assailing eyes,
Nor ope her lap to saint-seducing gold :
O, she is rich in beauty, only poor
That, when she dies, with beauty dies her store.[1]

Ben. Then she hath sworn that she will still live chaste?

Rom. She hath, and in that sparing makes huge waste;
For beauty, starved with her severity,
Cuts beauty off from all posterity.
She is too fair, too wise, wisely too fair,
To merit bliss by making me despair :
She hath forsworn to love; and in that vow
Do I live dead, that live to tell it now.

Ben. Be ruled by me, forget to think of her.

Rom. O, teach me how I should forget to think.

Ben. By giving liberty unto thine eyes;
Examine other beauties.

---

[1] That is, the beauty that she is rich in, will die with her, and that so her chief
wealth is a possession that she can not bequeath.

Rom.   'Tis the way
To call hers, exquisite, in question more :
He that is strucken blind cannot forget
The precious treasure of his eyesight lost :
Show me a mistress that is passing fair,
What doth her beauty serve but as a note
Where I may read who pass'd that passing fair ?
Farewell : thou canst not teach me to forget.
  Ben. Soft, I will go along.
  Rom. Tut, I have lost myself ; I am not here ;
This is not Romeo, he's some other where.   [*Exeunt.*

Enter CAPULET, PARIS, *and* PETER.

  Cap. But Montague is bound as well as I,
In penalty alike ; and 'tis not hard, I think,
For men so old as we to keep the peace.
  Par. Of honourable reckoning are you both ;
And pity 'tis you lived at odds so long.
But now, my lord, what say you to my suit ?
  Cap. But saying o'er what I have said before :
My child is yet a stranger in the world ;
She hath not seen the change of fourteen years :
Let two more summers wither in their pride
Ere we may think her ripe to be a bride.
  Par. Younger than she are happy mothers made.
  Cap. And too soon marr'd are those so early made.
The earth hath swallow'd all my hopes but she,
She is the hopeful lady of my earth :[1]
But woo her, gentle Paris, get her heart ;
· My will to her consent is but a part ;
An she agree, within her scope of choice
Lies my consent and fair according voice.
This night I hold an old accustom'd feast,

---

[1] Steevens regarded this expression, and perhaps rightly, as a translation of the French *fille de terre*—heiress.

Whereto I have invited many a guest,
Such as I love ; and you among the store,
Once more, most welcome, makes my number more.
At my poor house look to behold this night
Earth-treading stars that make dark heaven light :
Such comfort as do lusty young men feel
When well-apparell'd April on the heel
Of limping winter treads, even such delight
Among fresh female buds shall you this night
Inherit* at my house ; hear all, all see,
And like her most whose merit most shall be :
Which on more view, of many mine being one
May stand in number, though in reckoning none.
Come, go with me.   Go, sirrah, trudge about
Through fair Verona ; find those persons out
Whose names are written there and to them say,
My house and welcome on their pleasure stay.

[*Exeunt Capulet and Paris.*

Pet. Find them out whose names are written here ! It is
written that the shoemaker should meddle with his yard and the
tailor with his last, the fisher with his pencil and the painter with
his nets ; but I am sent to find those persons whose names are
here writ, and can never find what names the writing person hath
here writ.   I must to the learned.   In good time.

Enter BENVOLIO *and* ROMEO.

Ben. Tut, man, one fire burns out another's burning,
One pain is lessen'd by another's anguish :
Take thou some new infection to thy eye,
And the rank poison of the old will die.
Rom. Your plantain-leaf is excellent for that.
Ben. For what, I pray thee ?
Rom.   For your broken shin.
Ben. Why, Romeo, art thou mad ?
Rom. Not mad, but bound more than a madman is ;

Shut up in prison, kept without my food,
Whipt and tormented and—Good e'en, good fellow.
    Pet. God gi' good e'en.   I pray, sir, can you read?
    Rom. Ay, mine own fortune in my misery.
    Pet. Perhaps you have learned it without book: but, I pray, can
you read any thing you see?
    Rom. Ay, if I know the letters and the language.
    Pet. Ye say honestly: rest you merry!
    Rom. Stay, fellow; I can read.   [*Reads.*
    'Signor Martino and his wife and daughters; County Anselme
and his beauteous sisters; the lady widow of Vitruvio; Signor
Placentio and his lovely nieces; Mercutio and his brother Valen-
tine; mine uncle Capulet, his wife, and daughters; my fair niece
Rosaline; Livia; Signor Valentio and his cousin Tybalt; Lucio
and the lively Helena.'
A fair assembly: whither should they come?
    Pet. Up.
    Rom. Whither?
    Pet. To supper; to our house.
    Rom. Whose house?
    Pet. My master's.
    Rom. Indeed, I should have ask'd you that before.
    Pet. Now I'll tell you without asking: my master is the great
rich Capulet; and if you be not of the house of Montagues, I
pray, come and crush a cup of wine.   Rest you merry.   [*Exit.*
    Ben. At this same ancient feast of Capulet's
Sups the fair Rosaline whom thou so lovest,
With all the admired beauties of Verona:
Go thither, and with unattainted eye
Compare her face with some that I shall show,
And I will make thee think thy swan a crow.
    Rom. When the devout religion of mine eye
    Maintains such falsehood, then turn tears to fires;
And these, who, often drown'd, could never die,
    Transparent heretics, be burnt for liars!

One fairer than my love ! the all-seeing sun
Ne'er saw her match since first the world begun.
  Ben. Tut, you saw her fair, none else being by,
Herself poised with herself in either eye :
But in that crystal scales let there be weigh'd
Your lady's love against some other maid
That I will show you shining at this feast,
And she shall scant* show well that now seems best.
  Rom. I'll go along, no such sight to be shown,
But to rejoice in splendour of mine own.   [*Exeunt.*

Scene II. *A room in Capulet's house.*

Enter Lady Capulet *and* Nurse.

  La. Cap. Nurse, where's my daughter ? call her forth to me.
  Nurse. I bade her come. What, lamb ! what, lady-bird !—
Where's this girl ? What, Juliet !

Enter Juliet.

  Jul. How now ! who calls ?
  Nurse. Your mother.
  Jul. Madam, I am here. What is your will ?
  La. Cap. This is the matter. Nurse, give leave awhile,
We must talk in secret :—nurse, come back again ;
I have remember'd me, thou shalt hear our counsel.
Thou know'st my daughter's of a pretty age.
  Nurse. Faith, I can tell her age unto an hour.
  La. Cap. She's not fourteen.
  Nurse.   I'll lay fourteen of my teeth,—
And yet, to my teen* be it spoken, I have but four,—
She is not fourteen. How long is it now
To Lammas-tide ?
  La. Cap.   A fortnight and odd days.
  Nurse. Even or odd, of all days in the year,
Come Lammas-eve at night shall she be fourteen.

Susan and she—God rest all Christian souls !—
Were of an age : well, Susan is with God ;
She was too good for me :—but, as I said,
On Lammas-eve at night shall she be fourteen ;
That shall she, marry ; I remember it well.
'Tis since the earthquake now eleven years ;
And she was wean'd,—I never shall forget it—
Of all the days of the year, upon that day :
For then she could stand alone ; nay, by the rood,*
She could have run and waddled all about ;
For even the day before, she broke her brow :
I warrant, an I should live a thousand years,
I never should forget it.
    La. Cap. Enough of this ; I pray thee, hold thy peace.
    Nurse. Thou wast the prettiest babe that e'er I nursed :
An I might live to see thee married once,
I have my wish.
    La. Cap. Marry, that ' marry ' is the very theme
I came to talk of.   Tell me, daughter Juliet,
How stands your disposition to be married ?
    Jul. It is an honour that I dream not of.
    Nurse. An honour ! were not I thine only nurse,
I would say thou hadst suck'd wisdom from thy teat.
    La. Cap. Well, think of marriage now ; younger than you
Here in Verona, ladies of esteem,
Are made already mothers.   By my count,
I was your mother much upon these years
That you are now a maid.   Thus then in brief ;
The valiant Paris seeks you for his love.
    Nurse. A man, young lady ! lady, such a man
As all the world—why, he's a man of wax.
    La. Cap. Verona's summer hath not such a flower.
    Nurse. Nay, he's a flower ; in faith, a very flower.
    La. Cap. What say you ? can you love the gentleman ?
This night you shall behold him at our feast :
Read o'er the volume of young Paris' face,

And find delight writ there with beauty's pen ;
Examine every married lineament,
And see how one another lends content ;
And what obscured in this fair volume lies
Find written in the margent of his eyes.
Speak briefly, can you like of Paris' love?
    Jul. I 'll look to like, if looking liking move :
But no more deep will I endart mine eye
Than your consent gives strength to make it fly.

Enter PETER.

Pet. Madam, the guests are come, supper served up, you
called, my young lady asked for, the nurse cursed in the pantry,
and every thing in extremity.   I must hence to wait ; I beseech
you, follow straight.
    La. Cap. We follow thee.   [*Exit Peter.*]   Juliet, the county*
stays.   [*Exeunt.*

SCENE III.   *A street.*

Enter ROMEO, MERCUTIO, BENVOLIO, *and* Torch-bearers.

Rom. What, shall this speech be spoke for our excuse?
Or shall we on without apology ?
    Ben. The date is out of such prolixity :
We 'll have no Cupid hoodwink'd with a scarf,[1]

---

[1] The masque of ladies, or amazons, in Shakespeare's 'Timon,' is preceded by a
Cupid, who addresses the company in a speech.   This 'device' was a practice of courtly
life, before and during the time of Shakespeare.   But here he says—

                    'The date is out of such prolixity.'

    The 'Tartar's painted bow of lath,' is the bow of the Asiatic nations, with a
double curve, and Shakespeare employed the epithet to distinguish the bow of Cupid
from the old English long bow.   The 'crow-keeper,' who scares the ladies, had also a
bow.   He is the shuffle or mawkin—the scarecrow of rags and straw, with a bow and
arrow in his hand.   'That fellow handles his bow like a crow-keeper,' says Lear.   The
'without-book prologue faintly spoke after the prompter,' is supposed by Warton to
allude to the boy-actors that we afterward find so fully noticed in *Hamlet.*—KNIGHT.

Bearing a Tartar's painted bow of lath,
Scaring the ladies like a crow-keeper ;*
Nor no without-book prologue, faintly spoke
After the prompter, for our entrance :
But, let them measure us by what they will,
We'll measure them a measure,* and be gone.

Rom. Give me a torch :[1] I am not for this ambling ;
Being but heavy, I will bear the light.

Mer. Nay, gentle Romeo, we must have you dance.

Rom. Not I, believe me : you have dancing shoes
With nimble souls : I have a soul of lead
So stakes me to the ground, I cannot move.

Mer. You are a lover ; borrow Cupid's wings,
And soar with them above a common bound.

Rom. I am too sore enpierced with his shaft
To soar with his light feathers ; and so bound,
I cannot bound a pitch above dull woe :
Under love's heavy burthen do I sink.

Mer. And, to sink in it, should you burthen love ;
Too great oppression for a tender thing.

Rom. Is love a tender thing ? it is too rough,
Too rude, too boisterous, and it pricks like thorn.

Mer. If love be rough with you, be rough with love ;
Prick love for pricking, and you beat love down.
Give me a case to put my visage in :
A visor for a visor ! what care I
What curious eye doth quote* deformities ?
Here are the beetle-brows shall blush for me.

Ben. Come, knock and enter, and no sooner in
But every man betake him to his legs.

Rom. A torch for me : let wantons light of heart
Tickle the senseless rushes[2] with their heels ;

---

[1] See Note 1 on the following page.
[2] Carpets, though known in Italy, were not adapted to the English habits in the time
of Elizabeth ; and even the presence-chamber of that Queen was, according to Hentz-
ner, strewed with hay, by which he meant rushes. Mr. Brown, in his work on Shake-

For I am proverb'd with a grandsire phrase ;
I'll be a candle-holder,[1] and look on.
The game was ne'er so fair, and I am done.   .
  Mer. Tut, dun's the mouse,[2] the constable's own word :
If thou art dun, we'll draw thee from the mire
Of this sir-reverence[3] love, wherein thou stick'st
Up to the ears.   Come, we burn daylight, ho.
  Rom. Nay, that's not so.
  Mer.   I mean, sir, in delay
We waste our lights in vain, like lamps by day.
Take our good meaning, for our judgement sits
Five times in that ere once in our five wits.
  Rom. And we mean well, in going to this mask ;
But 'tis no wit to go.
  Mer.   Why, may one ask ?
  Rom. I dreamt a dream to-night.
  Mer.   And so did I.
  Rom. Well, what was yours ?
  Mer.   That dreamers often lie.
  Rom. In bed asleep, while they do dream things true.
  Mer. O, then, I see Queen Mab hath been with you.
She is the fairies' midwife, and she comes
In shape no bigger than an agate-stone

speare's autobiographical poems, says : ' The custom of strewing rushes in England
belonged also to Italy ; this may be seen in old authors, and their very word, *giuncare*,
now out of use, is a proof of it.'

 [1] Anciently, all rooms of state were lighted by waxen torches, borne in the hands of
attendants.   To hold the torch was not, however, a degrading office in England ; for the
gentlemen pensioners of Elizabeth held torches while a play was acted before her in the
chapel of King's College, Cambridge.

 [2] Of this proverbial expression, which is of not uncommon occurrence in old books,
no explanation worthy of notice has ever been offered.   In the next line the reference
is to a Christmas play called 'Dun is in the mire,' in which Dun was supposed to be
the name of a horse.—WHITE.

 [3] This was the old mode of apology for the introduction of a free expression.   Mercutio says, he will draw Romeo from ' the mire of this love,' and uses, parenthetically,
the ordinary form of apology for speaking so profanely of love.—KNIGHT.

  2

On the fore-finger of an alderman,
Drawn with a team of little atomies*
Athwart men's noses as they lie asleep :
Her waggon-spokes made of long spinners' legs ;
The cover, of the wings of grasshoppers ;
Her traces, of the smallest spider's web ;
Her collars, of the moonshine's watery beams ;
Her whip, of cricket's bone ; the lash, of film ;
Her waggoner, a small gray-coated gnat,
Not half so big as a round little worm
Prick'd from the lazy finger of a maid :
Her chariot is an empty hazel-nut,
Made by the joiner squirrel or old grub,
Time out o' mind the fairies' coachmakers.
And in this state she gallops night by night
Through lovers' brains, and then they dream of love ;
O'er courtiers' knees, that dream on court'sies straight ;
O'er lawyers' fingers, who straight dream on fees ;
O'er ladies' lips, who straight on kisses dream,
Which oft the angry Mab with blisters plagues,
Because their breaths with sweetmeats tainted are :
Sometime she gallops o'er a courtier's nose,
And then dreams he of smelling out a suit ; *
And sometime comes she with a tithe-pig's tail
Tickling a parson's nose as a' lies asleep,
Then he dreams of another benefice :
Sometime she driveth o'er a soldier's neck,
And then dreams he of cutting foreign throats,
Of breaches, ambuscadoes, Spanish blades,   .
Of healths five fathom deep ; and then anon
Drums in his ear, at which he starts and wakes,
And being thus frighted swears a prayer or two,
And sleeps again.   This is that very Mab —
    Rom. Peace, peace, Mercutio, peace !
Thou talk'st of nothing.

Mer.   True, I talk of dreams ;
Which are the children of an idle brain,
Begot of nothing but vain fantasy,
Which is as thin of substance as the air,
And more inconstant than the wind, who wooes
Even now the frozen bosom of the north,
And, being anger'd, puffs away from thence,
Turning his face to the dew-dropping south.

Ben. This wind you talk of blows us from ourselves ;
Supper is done, and we shall come too late.

Rom. I fear, too early : for my mind misgives
Some consequence, yet hanging in the stars,
Shall bitterly begin his fearful date
With this night's revels, and expire the term
Of a despised life closed in my breast,
By some vile forfeit of untimely death :
But He, that hath the steerage of my course,
Direct my sail !   On, lusty gentlemen.

Ben. Strike drum.   [*Exeunt.*

SCENE IV.   *A room in Capulet's house.*

Enter PETER, SAMPSON, *and other* Servants.

Pet. Where's Potpan, that he helps not to take away ? he shift
a trencher ! he scrape a trencher !

Sam. When good manners shall lie all in one or two men's
hands, and they unwashed too, 'tis a foul thing.

Pet. Away with the joint-stools, remove the court-cupboard,*
look to the plate.   Good thou, save me a piece of marchpane ;*
and, as thou lovest me, let the porter let in Susan Grindstone and
Nell.   Antony, and Potpan !

First Serv. Ay, boy, ready.

Pet. You are looked for and called for, asked for and sought for,
in the great chamber.

First Serv. We cannot be here and there too.

Pet. Cheerly, boys; be brisk awhile, and the longer liver take all. [*Exeunt all but Peter.*

Enter Musicians.

Pet. Musicians, O, musicians, O, play me some merry catch.

First Mus. Not a catch we.

Pet. You will not then?

First Mus. No.

Pet. I will then give it you soundly.

First Mus. What will you give us?

Pet. No money, on my faith, but the gleek;[1] I will give you the minstrel.

First Mus. Then will I give you the serving-creature.

Pet. Then will I lay the serving-creature's dagger on your pate. I will carry no crotchets; I'll re you, I'll fa you: do you note me?

First Mus. An you re us and fa us, you note us.

Sec. Mus. Pray you, put up your dagger, and put out your wit.

Pet. Then have at you with my wit! I will dry-beat you with an iron wit, and put up my iron dagger. Answer me like men:

'When griping grief the heart doth wound
    And doleful dumps the mind oppress,
  Then music with her silver sound'—

why 'silver sound'? why 'music with her silver sound'?— What say you, Simon Catling?*

First Mus. Marry, sir, because silver hath a sweet sound.

Pet. Pretty! What say you, Hugh Rebeck?*

Sec. Mus. I say, 'silver sound,' because musicians sound for silver.

Pet. Pretty too! What say you, James Soundpost?

---

[1] A pun is here intended. A *gleekman* or *gligman,* is a minstrel. *To give the gleek,* meant, also, to pass a jest upon a person, to make him appear ridiculous; a *gleek* being a jest or scoff.

Third Mus. Faith, I know not what to say.

Pet. O, I cry you mercy; you are the singer ː I will say for you. It is 'music with her silver sound,' because musicians have no gold for sounding:

> 'Then music with her silver sound
> With speedy help doth lend redress.'   [*Exit singing.*

First Mus. What a pestilent knave is this same.   [*Exeunt.*

SCENE V.   *A hall in Capulet's house.*

Enter CAPULET, *with* JULIET *and others of his house, meeting the* Guests, *and* Maskers.

Cap. Welcome, gentlemen! ladies that have their toes
·Unplagued with corns will have a bout with you:
Ah ha, my mistresses! which of you all
Will now deny to dance? she that makes dainty,
She, I'll swear, hath corns; am I come near ye now?
Welcome, gentlemen! I have seen the day
That I have worn a visor, and could tell
A whispering tale in a fair lady's ear,
Such as would please: 'tis gone, 'tis gone, 'tis gone:
You are welcome, gentlemen! Come, musicians, play.
A hall, a hall!* give room, and foot it, girls.
                              [*Music plays and they dance.*
More light, you knaves; and turn the tables up,
And quench the fire, the room is grown too hot.
Ah, sirrah, this unlook'd-for sport comes well.
Nay, sit, nay, sit, good cousin* Capulet;
For you and I are past our dancing days:
How long is't now since last yourself and I
Were in a mask?
    Sec. Cap.   By'r lady, thirty years.
    Cap. What, man! 'tis not so much, 'tis not so much:
'Tis since the nuptial of Lucentio,

Come Pentecost as quickly as it will,
Some five and twenty years ; and then we mask'd.
　　Sec. Cap. 'Tis more, 'tis more : his son is elder, sir;
His son is thirty.
　　Cap.　　　　　Will you tell me that ?
His son was but a ward two years ago.
　　Rom. [*To a Servingman*] What lady's that, which doth enrich
　　　　the hand
Of yonder knight ?
　　Serv.　　　　　I know not, sir.
　　Rom. O, she doth teach the torches to burn bright !
Her beauty hangs upon the cheek of night
Like a rich jewel in an Ethiope's ear ;
Beauty too rich for use, for earth too dear !
So shows a snowy dove trooping with crows,
As yonder lady o'er her fellows shows.
The measure* done, I'll watch her place of stand,
And, touching hers, make blessed my rude hand.
Did my heart love till now ? forswear it, sight !
For I ne'er saw true beauty till this night.
　　Tyb. This, by his voice, should be a Montague.
Fetch me my rapier, boy. [*To a Page*] What dares the slave
Come hither, cover'd with an antic face,
To fleer and scorn at our solemnity ?
Now, by the stock and honour of my kin,
To strike him dead I hold it not a sin.
　　Cap. Why, how now, kinsman ! wherefore storm you so ?
　　Tyb. Uncle, this is a Montague, our foe ;
A villain, that is hither come in spite,
To scorn at our solemnity this night.
　　Cap. Young Romeo is it ?
　　Tyb.　　　　　'Tis he, that villain Romeo.
　　Cap. Content thee, gentle coz, let him alone,
He bears him like a portly gentleman ;
And, to say truth, Verona brags of him

To be a virtuous and well-govern'd youth:
I would not for the wealth of all this town
Here in my house do him disparagement:
Therefore be patient, take no note of him:
It is my will, the which if thou respect,
Show a fair presence and put off these frowns,
An ill-beseeming semblance for a feast.

Tyb. It fits, when such a villain is a guest:
I'll not endure him.

Cap.   He shall be endured:
What, goodman boy! I say, he shall: go to;
Am I the master here, or you? go to.
You'll not endure him! God shall mend my soul,
You'll make a mutiny among my guests!
You will set cock-a-hoop!¹ you'll be the man!

Tyb. Why, uncle, 'tis a shame.

Cap.   Go to, go to;
You are a saucy boy: is't so, indeed?
This trick may chance to scathe* you, I know what:
You must contrary* me! marry, 'tis time.
Well said,* my hearts! You are a princox;* go:
Be quiet, or—More light, more light! For shame!
I'll make you quiet. What, cheerly, my hearts!
                                   [*They cease dancing.*

Tyb. Patience perforce with wilful choler meeting
Makes my flesh tremble in their different greeting.
I will withdraw: but this intrusion shall,
Now seeming sweet, convert to bitterest gall.   [*Exit.*

Rom. [*To Juliet*] If I profane with my unworthiest hand
    This holy shrine, the gentle sin is this,
  My lips, two blushing pilgrims, ready stand
    To smooth that rough touch with a tender kiss.

Jul. Good pilgrim, you do wrong your hand too much,

---

¹ May not this phrase have been originally 'cock-a-whoop?' the fitness of which
phrase, to express arrogant boasting, is plain.—WHITE.

Which mannerly devotion shows in this ;
For saints have hands that pilgrims' hands do touch,
And palm to palm is holy palmers'* kiss.

Rom. Have not saints lips, and holy palmers too ?

Jul. · Ay, pilgrim, lips that they must use in prayer.

Rom. O, then, dear saint, let lips do what hands do ;
They pray, grant thou, lest faith turn to despair.

Jul. Saints do not move, though grant for prayers' sake.

Rom. Then move not, while my prayer's effect I take.
Thus from my lips by thine my sin is purged.   [*Kissing her.*

Jul. Then have my lips the sin that they have took.

Rom. Sin from my lips ? O trespass sweetly urged !
Give me my sin again.

Jul.   You kiss by the book.

Nurse. Madam, your mother craves a word with you.

Rom. What is her mother ?

Nurse.   Marry, bachelor,
Her mother is the lady of the house,
And a good lady, and a wise and virtuous :
I nursed her daughter, that you talk'd withal ;
I tell you, he that can lay hold of her
Shall have the chinks.

Rom.   Is she a Capulet ?
O dear account ! my life is my foe's debt.

Ben. Away, be gone ; the sport is at the best.

Rom. Ay, so I fear ; the more is my unrest.

Cap. Nay, gentlemen, prepare not to be gone ;
We have a trifling foolish banquet towards.*
Is it e'en so ? why, then, I thank you all ; [*Guests take their leave.*
I thank you, honest gentlemen ; good night.
Come on then, by my fay, it waxes late :
I'l. to my rest.   [*Exeunt all but Juliet and Nurse.*

Jul. Come hither, nurse. What is yond gentleman ?

Nurse. The son and heir of old Tiberio.

Jul. What's he that now is going out of door ?

Nurse. Marry, that, I think, be young Petruchio.

Jul. What's he that follows there, that would not dance?

Nurse. I know not.

Jul. Go, ask his name.   If he be married,
My grave is like to be my wedding bed.

Nurse. His name is Romeo, and a Montague,
The only son of your great enemy.

Jul. My only love sprung from my only hate!
Too early seen unknown, and known too late!

                                        [*The curtain falls.*

ACT II.

SCENE I.   *A lane by the wall of Capulet's garden.*

Enter BENVOLIO *with* MERCUTIO.

Ben. Romeo! my cousin Romeo!

Mer.   He is wise;
And, on my life, hath stol'n him home to bed.

Ben. He ran this way, and leap'd this orchard wall:
Call, good Mercutio.

Mer.   Nay, I'll conjure too.
Romeo! humours! madman! passion! lover!
Appear thou in the likeness of a sigh:
Speak but one rhyme, and I am satisfied;
Cry but 'ay me!' pronounce but 'love' and 'dove;'
Speak to my gossip Venus one fair word,
One nick-name for her purblind son and heir,
Young auburn Cupid, he that shot so trim
When King Cophetua loved the beggar-maid!
He heareth not, he stirreth not, he moveth not;
The ape is dead, and I must conjure him.
I conjure thee by Rosaline's bright eyes,
By her high forehead and her scarlet lip,
That in thy likeness thou appear to us!

        2*

Ben. An if he hear thee, thou wilt anger him.

Mer. This cannot anger him : my invocation
Is fair and honest, and in his mistress' name,
I conjure only but to raise up him.

Ben. Come, he hath hid himself among these trees,
To be consorted with the humorous* night :
Blind is his love, and best befits the dark.

Mer. If love be blind, love cannot hit the mark.
Now will he sit under a medlar-tree,
And wish his mistress were that kind of fruit
As maids call medlars when they laugh alone.
Romeo, good night : I'll to my truckle-bed ;
This field-bed is too cold for me to sleep :
Come, shall we go ?

Ben.　　　　　　Go, then, for 'tis in vain
To seek him here that means not to be found.　　　[*Exeunt.*

Scene II.　*Capulet's garden.*

Enter Romeo.

Rom. He jests at scars that never felt a wound.
　　　　　　　　[*Juliet appears above at a window*
But, soft ! what light through yonder window breaks ?
It is the east, and Juliet is the sun !
It is my lady ; O, it is my love !
O, that she knew she were !
She speaks, yet she says nothing : what of that ?
Her eye discourses, I will answer it.
I am too bold, 'tis not to me she speaks :
Two of the fairest stars in all the heaven,
Having some business, do entreat her eyes
To twinkle in their spheres till they return.
What if her eyes were there, they in her head ?
The brightness of her cheek would shame those stars,

As daylight doth a lamp ; her eyes in heaven
Would through the airy region stream so bright
That birds would sing and think it were not night.
See, how she leans her cheek upon her hand!
O, that I were a glove upon that hand,
That I might touch that cheek !
   Jul.   Ah me !
   Rom.   She speaks :
O, speak again, bright angel ! for thou art
As glorious to this night, being o'er my head,
As is a winged messenger of heaven
Unto the white-upturned wondering eyes
Of mortals that fall back to gaze on him,
When he bestrides the lazy-pacing clouds
And sails upon the bosom of the air.
   Jul. O Romeo, Romeo ! wherefore art thou Romeo ?
Deny thy father and refuse thy name ;
Or, if thou wilt not, be but sworn my love,
And I'll no longer be a Capulet.
   Rom. [*Aside*] Shall I hear more, or shall I speak at this ?
   Jul. 'Tis but thy name that is my enemy.
What's in a name ? that which we call a rose
By any other name would smell as sweet ;
So Romeo would, were he not Romeo call'd,
Retain that dear perfection which he owes
Without that title.   Romeo, doff thy name,
And for thy name, which is no part of thee,
Take all myself.
   Rom.   I take thee at thy word :
Call me but love, and I'll be new baptized ;
Henceforth I never will be Romeo.
   Jul. What man art thou, that, thus bescreen'd in night,
So stumblest on my counsel ?
   Rom.   By a name
I know not how to tell thee who I am :

My name, dear saint, is hateful to myself,
Because it is an enemy to thee ;
Had I written, I would tear the word.

Jul. My ears have not yet drunk a hundred words
Of thy tongue's uttering, yet I know the sound :
Art thou not Romeo, and a Montague ?

Rom. Neither, fair maid, if either thee dislike.*

Jul. How camest thou hither, tell me, and wherefore?
The orchard walls are high and hard to climb,
And the place death, considering who thou art,
If any of my kinsmen find thee here.

Rom. With love's light wings did I o'er-perch these walls,
For stony limits cannot hold love out :
And what love can do, that dares love attempt ;
Therefore thy kinsmen are no stop to me.

Jul. If they do see thee, they will murder thee.

Rom. Alack, there lies more peril in thine eye
Than twenty of their swords : look thou but sweet,
And I am proof against their enmity.

Jul. I would not for the world they saw thee here.

Rom. I have night's cloak to hide me from their eyes ;
And but thou love me, let them find me here :
My life were better ended by their hate,
Than death prorogued,* wanting of thy love.

Jul. By whose direction found'st thou out this place ?

Rom. By love, that first did prompt me to inquire ;
He lent me counsel, and I lent him eyes.
I am no pilot ; yet, wert thou as far
As that vast shore wash'd with the farthest sea,
I would adventure for such merchandise.

Jul. Thou know'st the mask of night is on my face,
Else would a maiden blush bepaint my cheek
For that which thou hast heard me speak to-night.
Fain would I dwell on form, fain, fain deny
What I have spoke : but farewell compliment !

Dost thou love me? I know thou wilt say ' Ay,'
And I will take thy word : yet, if thou swear'st,
Thou mayst prove false : at lovers' perjuries,
They say, Jove laughs.   O gentle Romeo,
If thou dost love, pronounce it faithfully :
Or if thou think'st I am too quickly won,
I'll frown and be perverse and say thee nay,
So thou wilt woo ; but else, not for the world.
In truth, fair Montague, I am too fond ;
And therefore thou mayst think my 'haviour light :
But trust me, gentleman, I'll prove more true
Than those that have more cunning to be strange.*
I should have been more strange, I must confess,
But that thou overheard'st, ere I was 'ware,
My true love's passion : therefore pardon me,
And not impute this yielding to light love,
Which the dark night hath so discovered.
      Rom. Lady, by yonder blessed moon I swear,
That tips with silver all these fruit-tree tops,—
      Jul. O, swear not by the moon, th' inconstant moon,
That monthly changes in her circled orb,   •
Lest that thy love prove likewise variable.
      Rom. What shall I swear by ?
      Jul.   Do not swear at all ;
Or, if thou wilt, swear by thy gracious self,
Which is the god of my idolatry,
And I'll believe thee.
      Rom.   If my heart's dear love—
      Jul. Well, do not swear : although I joy in thee,
I have no joy of this contract to-night :
It is too rash, too unadvised, too sudden,
Too like the lightning, which doth cease to be
Ere one can say ' It lightens.'   Sweet, good night !
This bud of love, by summer's ripening breath,
May prove a beauteous flower when next we meet.

Good night, good night ! as sweet repose and rest
Come to thy heart as that within my breast !
   Rom. O, wilt thou leave me so unsatisfied ?
   Jul. What satisfaction canst thou have to-night ?
   Rom. The exchange of thy love's faithful vow for mine.
   Jul. I gave thee mine before thou didst request it :
And yet I would it were to give again.
   Rom. Wouldst thou withdraw it ? for what purpose, love ?
   Jul. But to be frank, and give it thee again.
And yet I wish but for the thing I have :
My bounty is as boundless as the sea,
My love as deep ; the more I give to thee,
The more I have, for both are infinite.
I hear some noise within ; dear love, adieu !   [*Nurse calls within.*
Anon, good nurse !   Sweet Montague, be true.
Stay but a little, I will come again.   [*Exit.*
   Rom. O blessed, blessed night !   I am afeard,
Being in night, all this is but a dream,
Too flattering-sweet to be substantial.

              Re-enter JULIET, *above.*

   Jul. Three words, dear Romeo, and good night indeed.
If that thy bent of love be honourable,
Thy purpose marriage, send me word to-morrow,
By one that I'll procure to come to thee,
Where and what time thou wilt perform the rite,
And all my fortunes at thy foot I'll lay
And follow thee my lord throughout the world.
   Nurse. [*Within*] Madam !
   Jul. I come, anon.—But if thou mean'st not well,
I do beseech thee—
   Nurse. [*Within*] Madam!
   Jul.   By and by, I come :—
To cease thy suit, and leave me to my grief :
To-morrow will I send.

Rom.   • So thrive my soul,—
Jul. A thousand times good night !   [*Exit.*
Rom. A thousand times the worse, to want thy light.
                                        [*Retiring slowly.*
                    Re-enter JULIET, *above.*

Jul. Hist ! Romeo, hist !—O, for a falconer's voice,
To lure this tassel-gentle* back again !
Bondage is hoarse, and may not speak aloud ;
Else would I tear the cave where Echo lies,
And make her airy tongue more hoarse than mine
With repetition of my Romeo's name.
Romeo !
  Rom. It is my soul that calls upon my name :
How silver-sweet sound lovers' tongues by night,
Like softest music to attending ears !
  Jul. Romeo !
  Rom.   My—
  Nurse. [*Within*] Madam !
  Jul.   At what o'clock to-morrow
Shall I send to thee ?
  Rom.   At the hour of nine.
  Jul. I will not fail : 'tis twenty years till then.
I have forgot why I did call thee back.
  Rom. Let me stand here till thou remember it.
  Jul. I shall forget, to have thee still stand there,
Remembering how I love thy company.
  Rom. And I'll still stay, to have thee still forget,
Forgetting any other home but this.
  Jul. 'Tis almost morning ; I would have thee gone :
And yet no farther than a wanton's bird,
Who lets it hop a little from her hand,
Like a poor prisoner in his twisted gyves,
And with a silk thread plucks it back again,
So loving-jealous of his liberty.
  Rom. I would I were thy bird.

Jul.   Sweet, so would I:
Yet I should kill thee with much cherishing.   [*Nurse calls within.*
Good night, good night! parting is such sweet sorrow
That I shall say good night till it be morrow.   [*Exeunt.*

SCENE III.   *Friar Laurence's cell.*

Enter FRIAR LAURENCE, *with a basket.*

Fri. L. The gray-eyed morn smiles on the frowning night,
Chequering the eastern clouds with streaks of light;
And flecked* darkness like a drunkard reels
From forth day's path and Titan's fiery wheels:
Now, ere the sun advance his burning eye,
The day to cheer and night's dank dew to dry,
I must up-fill this osier cage of ours
With baleful weeds and precious-juiced flowers.
O, mickle is the powerful grace that lies
In herbs, plants, stones, and their true qualities:
For nought so vile that on the earth doth live,
But to the earth some special good doth give;
Nor aught so good, but, strain'd from that fair use,
Revolts from true birth, stumbling on abuse:
Virtue itself turns vice, being misapplied,
And vice sometime's by action dignified.
Within the infant rind of this small flower
Poison hath residence, and medicine power:
For this, being smelt, with that part cheers each part,
Being tasted, slays all senses with the heart.
Two such opposed kings encamp them still
In man as well as herbs, grace and rude will;
And where the worser is predominant,
Full soon the canker death eats up that plant.

Enter ROMEO.

Rom. Good morrow, father!

Fri. L.   Benedicite!
What early tongue so sweet saluteth me?
Young son, it argues a distemper'd head
So soon to bid good morrow to thy bed:
Care keeps his watch in every old man's eye,
And where care lodges, sleep will never lie;
But where unbruised youth with unstuff'd brain
Doth couch his limbs, there golden sleep doth reign:
Therefore thy earliness doth me assure
Thou art up-roused by some distemperature;
Or if not so, then here I hit it right,
Our Romeo hath not been in bed to-night.
    Rom. That last is true; the sweeter rest was mine.
    Fri. L. God pardon sin! wast thou with Rosaline?
    Rom. With Rosaline, my ghostly father? no;
I have forgot that name, and that name's woe.
    Fri. L. That's my good son: but where hast thou been then?
    Rom. I'll tell thee ere thou ask it me again.
I have been feasting with mine enemy;
Where on a sudden one hath wounded me,
That's by me wounded: both our remedies
Within thy help and holy physic lies:
I bear no hatred, blessed man, for, lo,
My intercession likewise steads my foe.
    Fri. L. Be plain, good son, and homely in thy drift.
    Rom. Then plainly know my heart's dear love is set
On the fair daughter of rich Capulet:
As mine on hers, so hers is set on mine:
When, and where, and how,
We met, we woo'd and made exchange of vow,
I'll tell thee as we pass; but this I pray,
That thou consent to marry us to-day.
    Fri. L. Holy Saint Francis, what a change is here!
Is Rosaline, that thou didst love so dear,
So soon forsaken? young men's love then lies

Not truly in their hearts, but in their eyes.
And art thou changed? pronounce this sentence then:
Women may fall when there's no strength in men.

Rom. Thou chids't me off for loving Rosaline.

Fri. L. For doting, not for loving, pupil mine.

Rom. I pray thee, chide not: she whom I love now
Doth grace for grace and love for love allow;
The other did not so.

Fri. L.   O, she knew well
Thy love did read by rote and could not spell.
But come, young waverer, come, go with me,
In one respect I'll thy assistant be;
For this alliance may so happy prove,
To turn your households' rancour to pure love.

Rom. O, let us hence; I stand on sudden haste.

Fri. L. Wisely and slow; they stumble that run fast. [*Exeunt.*

SCENE IV. *A street.*

Enter BENVOLIO *and* MERCUTIO.

Mer. Where the devil should this Romeo be? Came he not
home to-night?

Ben. Not to his father's; I spoke with his man.

Mer. Ah, that same pale hard-hearted wench, that Rosaline,
Torments him so that he will sure run mad.

Ben. Tybalt, the kinsman of old Capulet,
Hath sent a letter to his father's house.

Mer. A challenge, on my life.

Ben. Romeo will answer it.

Mer. Any man that can write may answer a letter.

Ben. Nay, he will answer the letter's master, how he dares,
being dared.

Mer. Alas, poor Romeo, he is already dead! stabbed with a
white wench's black eye; shot through the ear with a love-song;

the very pin* of his heart cleft with the blind bow-boy's butt-shaft : and is he a man to encounter Tybalt ?

Ben. Why, what is Tybalt ?

Mer. More than prince of cats,[1] I can tell you. O, he's the courageous captain of complements. He fights as you sing prick-song,* keeps time, distance and proportion ; rests me his minim rest, one, two, and the third in your bosom : the very butcher of of a silk button, a duellist, a duellist ; a gentleman of the very first house, of the first and second cause :[2] ah, the immortal passado !* the punto reverso !* the hai !*

Ben. The what ?

Mer. The plague of such antic, lisping, affecting fantasticoes ;* these new tuners of accents ! A very good blade ! a very tall man ! a very good wench !' Why, is not this a lamentable thing, grandsire, that we should be thus afflicted with these strange flies, these fashion-mongers, these perdona-mi's, who stand so much on the new form that they cannot sit at ease on the old bench ?[3] O, their bones, their bones !

Ben. ·Here comes Romeo, here comes Romeo.

Mer. Without his roe, like a dried herring : O flesh, flesh, how art thou fishified ! Now·is he for the numbers that Petrarch flowed in : Laura to his lady was but a kitchen-wench ; marry, she had a better love to be-rhyme her ; Dido, a dowdy ; Cleopatra, a gipsy ; Helen and Hero, hildings and harlots ; ·Thisbe, a gray eye or so, but not to the purpose.

Enter ROMEO.

Signior Romeo, bon jour ! there's a French salutation to you. You gave us the counterfeit fairly last night.

---

[1] Tybert is the name given to the cat, in the old story of ' Reynard the Fox.'

[2] That is, one who understands the whole science of quarreling, and will tell you of the *first cause*, and the *second cause*, for which a man is to fight. The clown, in *As You Like It*, talks of the *seventh cause* in the same sense.

[3] During the ridiculous fashion which prevailed, of great 'bolstered breeches,' it is said, that it was necessary to cut away hollow places in the benches of the House of Commons, to make room for those monstrous protuberances, without which those *who stood on the new form* could not sit at ease on the old bench.

Rom. Good morrow to you both. What counterfeit did I give you?

Mer. The slip,* sir, the slip; can you not conceive?

Rom. Pardon, good Mercutio, my business was great; and in such a case as mine a man may strain courtesy.

Mer. That's as much as to say, Such a case as yours constrains a man to bow in the hams.

Rom. Meaning, to court'sy.

Mer. Thou hast most kindly hit it.

Rom. A most courteous exposition.

Mer. Nay, I am the very pink of courtesy.

Rom. Pink for flower.

Mer. Right.

Rom. Why, then is my pump well flowered.[1]

Mer. Well said: follow me this jest now, till thou hast worn out thy pump, that, when the single sole of it is worn, the jest may remain, after the wearing, solely singular.

Rom. O single-soled jest, solely singular for the singleness!

Mer. Come between us, good Benvolio; my wits faint.

Rom. Switch and spurs, switch and spurs; or I'll cry a match.

Mer. Nay, if thy wits run the wild-goose chase,[2] I have done; for thou hast more of the wild-goose in one of thy wits than, I am sure, I have in my whole five: was I with you there for the goose?

Rom. Thou wast never with me for any thing when thou wast not there for the goose.

Mer. I will bite thee by the ear for that jest.

Rom. Nay, good goose, bite not.

Mer. Thy wit is a very bitter sweeting;* it is a most sharp sauce.

---

[1] The ribbons in the pump were shaped as flowers.

[2] One kind of horse-race which resembled the flight of wild geese was formerl) known by this name. Two horses were started together, and whichever rider could ge the lead, the other was obliged to follow him, over whatever ground the foremo jockey chose to go. That horse which could distance the other won the race.

Rom. And is it not well served in to a sweet goose?

Mer. O, here's a wit of cheveril,* that stretches from an inch narrow to an ell broad!

Rom. I stretch it out for that word 'broad;' which added to the goose, proves thee far and wide a broad goose.

Mer. Why, is not this better now than groaning for love? now art thou sociable, now art thou Romeo; now art thou what thou art, by art as well as by nature: for this drivelling love is like a great natural, that runs lolling up and down to hide his bauble in a hole.

Ben. ˙A sail, a sail!

Mer. Two, two; a shirt, and a smock.

Enter Nurse *and* PETER.

Nurse. Peter!

Pet. Anon?

Nurse. My fan, Peter.

Mer. Good Peter, to hide her face; for her fan's the fairer of the two.

Nurse. God ye good morrow, gentlemen.

Mer. God ye good den,* fair gentlewoman.

Nurse. Out upon you! what a man are you!

Rom. One, gentlewoman, that God hath made himself to mar.

Nurse. By my troth, it is well said; 'for himself to mar,' quoth a'? Gentleman, can any of you tell me where I may find the young Romeo?

Rom. I can tell you; but young Romeo will be older when you have found him than he was when you sought him: I am the youngest of that name, for fault of a worse.

Nurse. You say well.

Mer. Yea, is the worst well? very well took, i'faith; wisely, wisely.

Nurse. If you be he, sir, I desire some confidence with you.

Ben. She will indite* him to some supper.

Mer. So ho!

Rom. What hast thou found?

Mer. No hare, sir; unless a hare, sir, in a lenten* pie, that is something stale and hoar ere it be spent.   Romeo, will you come to your ·father's? we'll to dinner thither.

Rom. I will follow you.

Mer. Farewell, ancient lady; farewell, [*singing*] 'lady, lady, lady.'   [*Exeunt Mercutio and Benvolio.*

Nurse. Marry, farewell! I pray you, sir, what saucy merchant was this, that was so full of his ropery?*

Rom. A gentleman, nurse, that loves to hear himself talk, and will speak more in a minute than he will stand to in a month.

Nurse. An a' speak any thing against me, I'll take him down, an a' were lustier than he is, and twenty such Jacks; and if I cannot, I'll find those that shall.   Scurvy knave!   I am none of his flirt-gills;* I am none of his skains-mates.* [*Turning to Peter*] And thou must stand by too, and suffer every knave to use me at his pleasure?

Pet. I saw no man use you at his pleasure; if I had, my weapon should quickly have been out, I warrant you: I dare draw as soon as another man, if I see occasion in a good quarrel and the law on my side.

Nurse. Now, afore God, I am so vexed that every part about me quivers.   Scurvy knave!   Pray you, sir, a word: and as I told you, my young lady bade me inquire you out; what she bade me say, I will keep to myself: but first let me tell ye, if ye should lead her into a fool's paradise, as they say, it were a very gross kind of behaviour, as they say: for the gentlewoman is young, and therefore, if you should deal double with her, truly it were an ill thing to be offered to any gentlewoman, and very weak dealing.

Rom. Nurse, commend me to thy lady and mistress.   I protest unto thee—

Nurse. Good heart, and, i' faith, I will tell her as much: Lord, Lord, she will be a joyful woman.

Rom. What wilt thou tell her, nurse? thou dost not mark me.

Nurse. I will tell her, sir, that you do protest; which, as I take it, is a gentlemanlike offer.

Rom. Bid her devise
Some means to come to shrift this afternoon;
And there she shall at Friar Laurence' cell
Be shrived and married. Here is for thy pains.

Nurse. No, truly, sir; not a penny.

Rom. Go to; I say you shall.

Nurse. This afternoon, sir? well, she shall be there.

Rom. And stay, good nurse, behind the abbey-wall:
Within this hour my man shall be with thee,
And bring thee cords made like a tackled stair;
Which to the high top-gallant of my joy
Must be my convoy in the secret night.
Farewell; be trusty, and I'll quite thy pains:
Farewell; commend me to thy mistress.

Nurse. Now God in heaven bless thee! Hark you, sir.

Rom. What say'st thou, my dear nurse?

Nurse. Is your man secret? Did you ne'er hear say,
Two may keep counsel, putting one away?

Rom. I warrant thee, my man's as true as steel.

Nurse. Well, sir; my mistress is the sweetest lady—Lord, Lord! when 'twas a little prating thing—O, there is a nobleman in town, one Paris, that would fain lay knife aboard; but she, good soul, had as lieve see a toad, a very toad, as see him. I anger her sometimes, and tell her that Paris is the properer man; but, I'll warrant you, when I say so, she looks as pale as any clout in the varsal world. Doth not rosemary and Romeo begin both with a letter?

Rom. Ay, nurse; what of that? both with an R.

Nurse. Ah, mocker! that's the dog's name; R is for the— No; I know it begins with some other letter—and she hath the prettiest sententious of it, of you and rosemary, that it would do you good to hear it.

Rom. Commend me to thy lady.

Nurse. Ay, a thousand times. [*Exit Romeo.*]   Peter!
Pet. Anon!
Nurse. Peter, take my fan, and go before, and apace. [*Exeunt.*

SCENE V. *Capulet's garden.*

Enter JULIET.

Jul. The clock struck nine when I did send the nurse;
In half an hour she promised to return.
Perchance she cannot meet him : that's not so.
O, she is lame ! love's heralds should be thoughts,
Which ten times faster glide than the sun's beams,
Driving back shadows over louring hills :
Therefore do nimble-pinion'd doves draw love,
And therefore hath the wind-swift Cupid wings.
Now is the sun upon the highmost hill
Of this day's journey, and from nine till twelve
Is three long hours ; yet she is not come.
Had she affections and warm youthful blood,
She would be as swift in motion as a ball ;
My words would bandy her to my sweet love,
And his to me :
O good, she comes !

Enter Nurse.

O honey nurse, what news ?
Hast thou met with him ?
Now, good sweet nurse,—O Lord, why look'st thou sad ?
Though news be sad, yet tell them merrily.
Nurse. I am a-weary ; give me leave awhile.
Fie, how my bones ache ! what a jaunce have I had !
Jul. I would thou hadst my bones and I thy news :
Nay, come, I pray thee, speak ; good, good nurse, speak.
Is thy news good, or bad ? answer to that ;
Say either, and I'll stay the circumstance :
Let me be satisfied, is't good or bad ?

Nurse. Well, you have made a simple choice; you know not
how to choose a man: Go thy ways, wench; serve God.   What,
have you dined at home?

Jul. What says he of our marriage? what of that?

Nurse. Lord, how my head aches! what a head have I!
It beats as it would fall in twenty pieces.
My back o' t' other side,—ah, my back, my back!
Beshrew your heart for sending me about,
To catch my death with jauncing up and down!

Jul. I' faith, I am sorry that thou art not well.
Sweet, sweet, sweet nurse, tell me, what says my love?

Nurse. Your love says, like an honest gentleman, and a courteous, and a kind, and a handsome, and, I warrant, a virtuous,—
Where is your mother?

Jul. Where is my mother! why, she is within;
Where should she be?   How oddly thou repliest!
' Your love says like an honest gentleman,
Where is your mother?'

Nurse. Are you so hot? marry, come up, I trow;
Is this the poultice for my aching bones?
Henceforward do your messages yourself.

Jul. Here's such a coil! come, what says Romeo?

Nurse. Have you got leave to go to shrift* to-day?

Jul. I have.

Nurse. Then hie you hence to Friar Laurence' cell;
There stays a husband to make you a wife:
Now comes the wanton blood up in your cheeks,
They'll be in scarlet straight at any news.
Hie you to church; I must another way,
To fetch a ladder, by the which your love
Must climb a bird's nest soon when it is dark:
Go, I'll to dinner; hie you to the cell.

Jul. Hie to high fortune!   Honest nurse, farewell.   [*Exeunt.*

3

SCENE VI. *Friar Laurence's cell.*

Enter FRIAR LAURENCE *and* ROMEO.

Fri. L. So smile the heavens upon this holy act
That after-hours with sorrow chide us not !

Rom. Amen, amen ! but come what sorrow can,
It cannot countervail* the exchange of joy
That one short minute gives me in her sight :
Do thou but close our hands with holy words,
Then love-devouring death do what he dare,
It is enough I may but call her mine.

Fri. L. These violent delights have violent ends
And in their triumph die, like fire and powder
Which as they kiss consume : the sweetest honey
Is loathsome in his own deliciousness
And in the taste confounds the appetite :
Therefore, love moderately ; long love doth so ;
Too swift arrives as tardy as too slow.
Here comes the lady.

Enter JULIET.

O, so light a foot
Will ne'er wear out the everlasting flint.
A lover may bestride the gossamer
That idles in the wanton summer air,
And yet not fall ; so light is vanity.

Jul. Good even to my ghostly confessor.

Fri. L. Romeo shall thank thee, daughter, for us both

Jul. As much to him, else is his thanks too much.

Rom. Ah, Juliet, if the measure of thy joy
Be heap'd like mine, and that thy skill be more
To blazon it, then sweeten with thy breath
This neighbour air, and let rich music's tongue
Unfold the imagined happiness that both
Receive in either by this dear encounter.

Jul. Conceit,* more rich in matter than in words,

Brags of his substance, not of ornament :
They are but beggars that can count their worth ;
But my true love is grown to such excess,
I cannot sum up sum of half my wealth.

Fri. L. Come, come with me, and we will make short work ;
For, by your leaves, you shall not stay alone
Till holy church incorporate two in one.   [*Exeunt.*

SCENE VII. *A public place.*

Enter MERCUTIO, BENVOLIO, *and a* Page.

Ben. I pray thee, good Mercutio, let's retire :
The day is hot, the Capulets abroad,
And, if we meet, we shall not 'scape a brawl ;
For now these hot days is the mad blood stirring.

Mer. Thou art like one of those fellows that when he enters
the confines of a tavern claps me his sword upon the table, and
says ' God send me no need of thee !' and by the operation of the
second cup draws it on the drawer, when indeed there is no need.

Ben. Am I like such a fellow?

Mer. Come, come, thou art as hot a Jack in thy mood as any
in Italy, and as soon moved to be moody and as soon moody to be
moved.

Ben. And what to ?

Mer. Nay, an there were two such, we should have none
shortly, for one would kill the other. Thou ! why, thou wilt
quarrel with a man that hath a hair more, or a hair less, in his
beard than thou hast : thou wilt quarrel with a man for cracking
nuts, having no other reason but because thou hast hazel eyes ;
what eye, but such an eye, would spy out such a quarrel ? thy
head is as full of quarrels as an egg is full of meat, and yet thy
head hath been beaten as addle as an egg for quarrelling : thou
hast quarrelled with a man for coughing in the street, because he
hath wakened thy dog that hath lain asleep in the sun : didst thou

not fall out with a tailor for wearing his new doublet before Easter ? with another, for tying his new shoes with old riband ? and yet thou wilt tutor me from quarrelling !

Ben. An I were so apt to quarrel as thou art, any man should buy the fee-simple of my life for an hour and a quarter.

Mer. The fee-simple ! O simple !

Ben. By my head, here come the Capulets.

Mer. By my heel, I care not.

Enter TYBALT *and others.*

Tyb. Follow me close, for I will speak to them.
Gentlemen, good den : a word with one of you.

Mer. And but one word with one of us ? couple it with some-thing ; make it a word and a blow.

Tyb. You shall find me apt enough to that, sir, an you will give me occasion.

Mer. Could you not take some occasion without giving ?

Tyb. Mercutio, thou consort'st with Romeo,—

Mer. Consort !* what, dost thou make us minstrels ? an thou make minstrels of us, look to hear nothing but discords : here's my fiddlestick ; here's that shall make you dance. 'Zounds, consort !

Ben. We talk here in the public haunt of men :
Either withdraw unto some private place,
Or reason coldly of your grievances,
Or else depart ; here all eyes gaze on us.

Mer. Men's eyes were made to look, and let them gaze ;
I will not budge for no man's pleasure, I.

Tyb. Well, peace be with you, sir : here comes my man.

Mer. But I'll be hang'd, sir, if he wear your livery :
Marry, go before to field, he'll be your follower ;
Your worship in that sense may call him man.

Enter ROMEO.

Tyb. Romeo, the love I bear thee can afford
No better term than this,—thou art a villain.

Rom. Tybalt, the reason that I have to love thee
Doth much excuse the appertaining rage
To such a greeting : villain am I none ;
Therefore farewell ; I see thou know'st me not.

Tyb. Boy, this shall not excuse the injuries
That thou hast done me ; therefore turn and draw.

Rom. I do protest, I never injured thee,
But love thee better than thou canst devise
Till thou shalt know the reason of my love :
And so, good Capulet,—which name I tender
As dearly as mine own,—be satisfied.

Mer. O calm, dishonourable, vile submission !
Alla stoccata* carries it away.   [*Draws.*
Tybalt, you rat-catcher, will you walk ?

Tyb. What wouldst thou have with me ?

Mer. Good king of cats, nothing but one of your nine lives,
that I mean to make bold withal, and, as you shall use me hereafter, dry-beat the rest of the eight.   Will you pluck your sword
out of his pilcher* by the ears ? make haste, lest mine be about
your ears ere it be out.

Tyb. I am for you.   [*Drawing.*

Rom. Gentle Mercutio, put thy rapier up.

Mer. Come, sir, your passado.   [*They fight.*

Rom. Draw, Benvolio ; beat down their weapons.
Gentlemen, for shame, forbear this outrage !
Tybalt, Mercutio, the prince expressly hath
Forbid bandying in Verona streets :
Hold, Tybalt! good Mercutio !   [*Tybalt under Romeo's arm stabs
                         Mercutio and flies with his followers.*

Mer.   I am hurt ;
A plague o' both the houses ! I am sped :*
Is he gone, and hath nothing?

Ben.   What, art thou hurt ?

Mer. Ay, ay, a scratch, a scratch ; marry, 'tis enough.
Where is my page ?   Go, villain, fetch a surgeon.   [*Exit Page.*

Rom. Courage, man ; the hurt cannot be much.

Mer. No, 'tis not so deep as a well, nor so wide as a church-door; but 'tis enough, 'twill serve: ask for me to-morrow, and you shall find me a grave man. I am peppered, I warrant, for this world. A plague o' both your houses! 'Zounds, a dog, a rat, a mouse, a cat, to scratch a man to death! a braggart, a rogue, a villain, that fights by the book of arithmetic! Why the devil came you between us? I was hurt under your arm.

Rom. I thought all for the best.

Mer. Help me into some house, Benvolio,
Or I shall faint. A plague o' both your houses!
They have made worms' meat of me : I have it,
And soundly too : your houses! [*Exeunt Mercutio and Benvolio.*

Rom. This gentleman, the prince's near ally,
My very friend, hath got his mortal hurt
In my behalf; my reputation stain'd
With Tybalt's slander,—Tybalt, that an hour
Hath been my kinsman: O sweet Juliet,
Thy beauty hath made me effeminate,
And in my temper soften'd valour's steel!

BENVOLIO, *from the house.*

Ben. O Romeo, Romeo, brave Mercutio's dead!
That gallant spirit hath aspired the clouds,
Which too untimely here did scorn the earth.
Here comes the furious Tybalt back again.

Rom. Alive, in triumph! and Mercutio slain!
Away to heaven, respective* lenity,
And fire-eyed fury be my conduct* now!

Re-enter TYBALT *and* BENVOLIO.

Rom. Now, Tybalt, take the 'villain' back again
That late thou gavest me ; for Mercutio's soul
Is but a little away above our heads,
Staying for thine to keep him company :

Either thou, or I, or both, must go with him.

Tyb. Thou, wretched boy, that didst consort him here,
Shalt with him hence.

Rom.   This shall determine that.

                                    [*They fight ; Tybalt falls*

Ben. Romeo, away, be gone !
The citizens are up, and Tybalt slain :
Stand not amazed : the prince will doom thee death
If thou art taken : hence, be gone, away !

Rom. O, I am fortune's fool !   [*Exeunt*

ACT III.

Scene I. *An apartment in Capulet's house.*

Enter Juliet.

Jul. Gallop apace, you fiery-footed steeds,
Towards Phœbus' lodging : such a waggoner
As Phaeton would whip you to the west,
And bring in cloudy night immediately.
Spread thy close curtain, love-performing night,
That rumour's[1] eyes may wink, and Romeo
Leap to these arms, untalk'd of and unseen.
Come night, come, Romeo, come, thou day in night ;
For thou wilt lie upon the wings of night
Whiter than new snow on a raven's back.
Come, gentle night, come, loving, black-brow'd night,
Give me my Romeo ; and, when he shall die,

---

[1] In the original 'runaway's'—an expression which none of the commentators have been able to explain to their own satisfaction or that of their readers. The substitute we have adopted commends itself to our judgment as the best that has been suggested. It at least has the merit of giving sense and consistency to the passage, a merit which none of the others has. Juliet bids the night spread her close curtain, that, the eyes of rumor being closed, Romeo may leap to her arms 'untalked of and unseen.'—Editor

Take him and cut him out in little stars,
And he will make the face of heaven so fine
That all the world will be in love with night
And pay no worship to the garish sun.
O, I have bought the mansion of a love,
But not possess'd it ; so tedious is this day
As is the night before some festival
To an impatient child that hath new robes
And may not wear them.   O, here comes my nurse,
And she brings news, and every tongue that speaks
But Romeo's name speaks heavenly eloquence.

Enter Nurse.

Now, nurse, what news ?
Ay me ! what news ? why dost thou wring thy hands ?
  Nurse. Ah, well-a-day ! he's dead, he's dead, he's dead.
We are undone, lady, we are undone.
Alack the day ! he's gone, he's kill'd, he's dead.
  Jul. Can heaven be so envious ?*
  Nurse.   .   Romeo can,
Though heaven cannot.   O Romeo, Romeo !
Who ever would have thought it ?   Romeo !
  Jul. What devil art thou that dost torment me thus ?
This torture should be roar'd in dismal hell.
Hath Romeo slain himself ? say thou but ' I,' [1]
And that bare vowel ' I ' shall poison more
Than the death-darting eye of cockatrice.
  Nurse. I saw the wound, I saw it with mine eyes—
God save the mark ! [2] here on his manly breast :

[1] It is here necessary to retain the old spelling of the affirmative particle I (ay).

[2] Of this exclamation, so common in Shakespeare's day, the origin and the meaning have yet to be discovered.   But may not this passage aid the search ?   For in the 4to of 1597 it stands, 'God save the *sample !'*   May we conclude from this that in the other phrase 'mark' means such a mark as is made with a needle upon a sampler ?— WHITE.

A piteous corse, a bloody piteous corse ;
Pale, pale as ashes, all bedaub'd in blood,
All in gore blood : I swounded at the sight.

Jul. O, break, my heart ! poor bankrupt, break at once !
To prison, eyes, ne'er look on liberty !
Vile earth, to earth resign, end motion here,
And thou and Romeo press one heavy bier !   •

Nurse. O Tybalt, Tybalt, the best friend I had !
O courteous Tybalt ! honest gentleman !
That ever I should live to see thee dead !

Jul. What storm is this that blows so contrary ?
Is Romeo slaughter'd, and is Tybalt dead ?
My dear-loved cousin, and my dearer lord ?
Then, dreadful trumpet, sound the general doom !
For who is living, if those two are gone ?

Nurse. Tybalt is gone, and Romeo banished ;
Romeo that kill'd him, he is banished.

Jul. O God ! did Romeo's hand shed Tybalt's blood ?

Nurse. It did, it did ; alas the day, it did !

Jul. O nature, what hadst thou to do in hell,
When thou didst bower the spirit of a fiend
In mortal paradise of such sweet flesh ?
Was ever book containing such vile matter
So fairly bound ?   O, that deceit should dwell
In such a gorgeous palace !

Nurse. ·   There's no trust,
No faith, no honesty in men ; all perjured,
All forsworn, all naught, all dissemblers.
Shame come to Romeo !

Jul.   Blister'd be thy tongue
For such a wish ! he was not born to shame :
Upon his brow shame is ashamed to sit ;
For 'tis a throne where honour may be crown'd
Sole monarch of the universal earth.
O, what a beast was I to chide at him !

9*

Nurse. Will you speak well of him that kill'd your cousin?
Jul. Shall I speak ill of him that is my husband?
Ah, poor my lord, what tongue shall smooth* thy name,
When I, thy three-hours wife, have mangled it?
Back, foolish tears, back to your native spring;
Your tributary drops belong to woe,
Which you mistaking offer up to joy.
My husband lives, that Tybalt would have slain;
And Tybalt's dead, that would have slain my husband:
All this is comfort; wherefore weep I then?
Some word there was, worser than Tybalt's death,
That murder'd me: I would forget it fain;
But, O, it presses to my memory,
Like damned guilty deeds to sinners' minds:
' Tybalt is dead and, Romeo banished;'
That ' banished,' that one word ' banished,'
Hath slain ten thousand Tybalts.   To speak that word,
Is father, mother, Tybalt, Romeo, Juliet, all slain, all dead.
Where is my father, and my mother, nurse?
Nurse. Weeping and wailing over Tybalt's corse:
Will you go to them?   I will bring you thither.
Jul. Wash they his wounds with tears: mine shall be spent,·
When theirs are dry, for Romeo's banishment.
Nurse. Hie to your chamber: I'll find Romeo
To comfort you: I wot well where he is.
Hark ye, your Romeo will be here at night:
I'll to him; he is hid at Laurence' cell.
Jul. O, find him! give this ring to my true knight,
And bid him come to take his last farewell.   [*Exeunt.*

SCENE II.   *Friar Laurence's cell.*

Enter FRIAR LAURENCE.

Fri. L. Romeo, come forth; come forth, thou fearful man:

Affliction is enamour'd of thy parts,
And thou art wedded to calamity.

Enter ROMEO.

Rom. Father, what news? what is the prince's doom?
What sorrow craves acquaintance at my hand,
That I yet know not.
 Fri. L.   Too familiar
Is my dear son with such sour company:
I bring thee tidings of the prince's doom.
 Rom. What less than dooms-day is the prince's doom?
 Fri. L. A gentler judgement vanish'd from his lips,
Not body's death, but body's banishment.
 Rom. Ha, banishment! be merciful, say 'death;'
For exile hath more terror in his look,
Much more than death: do not say 'banishment.'
 Fri. L. Here from Verona art thou banished:
Be patient, for the world is broad and wide.
 Rom. There is no world without Verona walls, .
But purgatory, torture, hell itself.
Hence banished is banish'd from the world,
And world's exile is death: then 'banished'
Is death mis-term'd: calling death 'banished,'
Thou cutt'st my head off with a golden axe
And smilest upon the stroke that murders me.
 Fri. L. O deadly sin! O rude unthankfulness!
Thy fault our law calls death; but the kind prince,
Taking thy part, hath rush'd* aside the law,
And turn'd that black word death to banishment:
This is dear mercy, and thou seest it not.
 Rom. 'Tis torture, and not mercy: heaven is here,
Where Juliet lives; and every cat and dog
And little mouse, every unworthy thing,
Live here in heaven and may look on her,
But Romeo may not: more validity,*

More honourable state, more courtship lives
In carrion-flies than Romeo : they may seize
On the white wonder of dear Juliet's hand,
And steal immortal blessing from her lips :
Hadst thou no poison mix'd, no sharp-ground knife,
No sudden mean of death, though ne'er so mean,
But 'banished' to kill me ?—'Banished'?
O friar, the damned use that word in hell ;
Howling attends it : how hast thou the heart,
Being a divine, a ghostly confessor,
A sin-absolver, and my friend profess'd,
To mangle me with that word 'banished'?

   Fri. L. Thou fond mad man, hear me but speak a word.
   Rom. O, thou wilt speak again of banishment.
   Fri. L. I'll give thee armour to keep off that word ;
Adversity's sweet milk, philosophy,
To comfort thee, though thou art banished.
   Rom. Yet 'banished'?   Hang up philosophy !
Unless philosophy can make a Juliet,
Displant a town, reverse a prince's doom,
It helps not, it prevails not : talk no more.
   Fri. L. Let me dispute with thee of thy estate.
   Rom. Thou canst not speak of that thou dost not feel :
Wert thou as young as I, Juliet thy love,
An hour but married, Tybalt murdered,
Doting like me, and like me banished,
Then mightst thou speak, then mightst thou tear thy hair,
And fall upon the ground, as I do now,
Taking the measure of an unmade grave.   [*Knocking within.*
   Fri. L. Arise ; one knocks ; good Romeo, hide thyself.
                                     [*Knocking.*
Hark, how they knock ! Who's there ? Romeo, arise ;
Thou wilt be taken.—Stay awhile !—Stand up ;   [*Knocking.*
Run to my study.—By and by !—God's will,
What simpleness is this !—I come, I come !   [*Knocking.*

Who knocks so hard? whence come you? what's your will?
  Nurse. [*Within*] Let me come in, and you shall know my
      errand;
I come from Lady Juliet.
  Fri. L.   Welcome, then.

           .   *Enter* Nurse.

  Nurse. O holy friar, O, tell me, holy friar,
Where is my lady's lord, where's Romeo?
  Fri. L. There on the ground, with his own tears made drunk.
  Nurse. O, he is even in my mistress' case,
Just in her case!
  Fri. L.   O woeful sympathy!
Piteous predicament!
  Nurse.   Even so lies she,
Blubbering and weeping, weeping and blubbering.
Stand up, stand up; stand, an you be a man:
For Juliet's sake, for her sake, rise and stand.
  Rom. Nurse!
  Nurse. Ah sir! ah sir! Well, death's the end of all.
  Rom. Speakest thou of Juliet! how is it with her?
Doth she not think me an old murderer,
Now I have stain'd the childhood of our joy
With blood removed but little from her own?
Where is she? and how doth she? and what says
My conceal'd lady to our cancell'd love?
  Nurse. O, she says nothing, sir, but weeps and weeps;
And now falls on her bed; and then starts up,
And Tybalt calls; and then on Romeo cries,
And then down falls again.
  Rom.   As if that name,
Shot from the deadly level of a gun,
Did murder her; as that name's cursed hand
Murder'd her kinsman. O, tell me, friar, tell me,
In what vile part of this anatomy

Doth my name lodge? tell me, that I may sack
The hateful mansion.   [*Draws his sword.*
   Fri. L.   Hold thy desperate hand:
Art thou a man? thy form cries out thou art:
Thy tears are womanish; thy wild acts denote
The unreasonable fury of a beast:
Unseemly woman in seeming man!   `
Or ill-beseeming beast in seeming both!
Thou hast amazed me: by my holy order,
I thought thy disposition better temper'd.
Hast thou slain Tybalt? wilt thou slay thyself?
And slay thy lady that in thy life lives,
By doing damned hate upon thyself?
What, rouse thee, man! thy Juliet is alive,
For whose dear sake thou wast but lately dead;
There art thou happy: Tybalt would kill thee,
But thou slew'st Tybalt; there art thou happy too;
The law, that threaten'd death, became thy friend,
And turns it to exile; there art thou happy:
A pack of blessings lights upon thy back;
Happiness courts thee in her best array;
But, like a misbehaved and sullen wench,
Thou pout'st upon thy fortune and thy love:
Take heed, take heed, for such die miserable.
Go, get thee to thy love, as was decreed,
Ascend her chamber, hence and comfort her:
But look thou stay not till the watch be set,
For then thou canst not pass to Mantua;
Where thou shalt live till we can find a time
To blaze your marriage, reconcile your friends,
Beg pardon of thy prince and call thee back
With twenty hundred thousand times more joy
Than thou went'st forth in lamentation.
Go before, nurse: commend me to thy lady,
And bid her hasten all the house to bed,

Which heavy sorrow makes them apt unto :
Romeo is coming.

Nurse. O Lord, I could have stay'd here all the night
To hear good counsel : O, what learning is !
My lord, I'll tell my lady you will come.

Rom. Do so, and bid my sweet prepare to chide.

Nurse. Here, sir, a ring she bid me give you, sir :
Hie you, make haste, for it grows very late.   [*Exit.*

Rom. How well my comfort is revived by this !

Fri. L. Go hence ; good night ; and here stands all your state :
Either be gone before the watch be set,
Or by the break of day disguised from hence :
Sojourn in Mantua ; I'll find out your man,
And he shall signify from time to time
Every good hap to you that chances here :
Give me thy hand ; 'tis late : farewell ; good night.

Rom. But that a joy past joy calls out on me,
It were a grief, so brief to part with thee :
Farewell.   [*Exeunt.*

SCENE III. *A room in Capulet's house.*

Enter CAPULET, LADY CAPULET, *and* PARIS.

Cap. Things have fall'n out, sir, so unluckily
That we have had no time to move our daughter.
Look you, she loved her kinsman Tybalt dearly,
And so did I.   Well, we were born to die.
'Tis very late ; she's not come down to-night :
I promise you, but for your company,
I would have been a-bed an hour ago.

Par. These times of woe afford no time to woo.
Madam, good night : commend me to your daughter.

La. Cap. I will, and know her mind early to-morrow ;
To-night she's mew'd* up to her heaviness.

Cap. Sir Paris, I will make a desperate* tender
Of my child's love : I think she will be ruled
In all respects by me ; nay more, I doubt it not.
Wife, go you to her ere you go to bed;
Acquaint her here of my son Paris' love ; '
And bid her, mark you me, on Wednesday next—
But, soft ! what day is this ?
    Par.   Monday, my lord.
    Cap. Monday ! ha, ha ! Well, Wednesday is too soon ;
O' Thursday let it be : o' Thursday, tell her,
She shall be married to this noble earl.
Will you be ready ? do you like this haste ?
We'll keep no great ado ; a friend or two ;
For, hark you, Tybalt being slain so late,
It may be thought we held him carelessly,
Being our kinsman, if we revel much :
Therefore we'll have some half-a-dozen friends,
And there an end. But what say you to Thursday ?
    Par. My lord, I would that Thursday were to-morrow.
    Cap. Well, get you gone : o' Thursday be it then.
Go you to Juliet ere you go to bed,
Prepare her, wife, against this wedding-day.
Farewell, my lord. Light to my chamber, ho !
Afore me, it is so very very late
That we may call it early by and by :
Good night.   [*Exeunt.*

SCENE IV. *Loggia to Juliet's chamber.*

ROMEO *and* JULIET *discovered.*

Jul. Wilt thou be gone ? it is not yet near day:
It was the nightingale, and not the lark,
That pierced the fearful hollow of thine ear ;

Nightly she sings on yond pomegranate-tree ;
Believe me, love, it was the nightingale.
   Rom. It was the lark, the herald of the morn,
No nightingale : look, love, what envious streaks
Do lace the severing clouds in yonder east :
Night's candles are burnt out, and jocund day
Stands tiptoe on the misty mountain tops :
I must be gone and live, or stay and die.
   Jul. Yond light is not day-light, I know it, I :   •
It is some meteor that the sun exhales,
To be to thee this night a torch-bearer,
And light thee on thy way to Mantua :
Therefore stay yet ; thou need'st not to be gone.
   Rom. Let me be ta'en, let me be put to death ;
I am content, so thou wilt have it so.
I'll say yon grey is not the morning's eye,
'Tis but the pale reflex of Cynthia's brow ;
Nor that is not the lark, whose notes do beat
The vaulty heaven so high above our heads :
I have more care to stay, than will to go :
Come, death, and welcome ! Juliet wills it so.
How is't, my soul ? let's talk : it is not day.
   Jul. It is, it is : hie hence, be gone, away !
It is the lark that sings so out of tune,
Straining harsh discords and unpleasing sharps.
Some say the lark makes sweet division ;*
This doth not so, for she divideth us :
Some say the lark and loathed toad change eyes ;
O, now I would they had changed voices too !
Since arm from arm that voice doth us affray,
Hunting thee hence with hunts-up* to the day.
O, now be gone ; more light and light it grows.
   Rom. More light and light : more dark and dark our woes !

Enter Nurse, *to the chamber.*

Nurse. Madam!

Jul. Nurse?

Nurse. Your lady mother is coming to your chamber :
The day is broke ; be wary, look about.   [*Exit.*

  Rom. Farewell, farewell ! one kiss, and I'll descend. [*Descends.*

  Jul. Art thou gone so ? my lord, my love, my friend !
I must hear from thee every day in the hour,
For in a minute there are many days :
O, by this count I shall be much in years
Ere I again behold my Romeo.   ·

  Rom. Farewell !
I will omit no opportunity
That may convey my greetings, love, to thee.

  Jul. O, think'st thou we shall ever meet again ?

  Rom. I doubt it not ; and all these woes shall serve
For sweet discourses in our time to come.

  Jul. O God ! I have an ill-divining soul.
Methinks I see thee, now thou art below,
As one dead in the bottom of a tomb :
Either my eyesight fails or thou look'st pale.

  Rom. And trust me, love, in my eye so do you :
Dry sorrow drinks our blood.   Adieu, adieu !   [*Exit.*

  Jul. O fortune, fortune ! all men call thee fickle :
If thou art fickle, what dost thou with him
That is renown'd for faith ?   Be fickle, fortune ;
For then, I hope, thou wilt not keep him long,
But send him back.

  La. Cap. [*Within*] Ho, daughter ! are you up ?

  Jul. Who is 't that calls ? it is my lady mother !
Is she not down so late, or up so early ?
What unaccustom'd cause procures* her hither ?

Enter LADY CAPULET.

  La. Cap. Why, how now, Juliet !

Jul.   ⋅   Madam, I am not well.

La. Cap. Evermore weeping for your cousin's death?
What, wilt thou wash him from his grave with tears?
An if thou couldst, thou couldst not make him live ;
Therefore have done : some grief shows much of love,
But much of grief shows still some want of wit.
But now I'll tell thee joyful tidings, girl.

Jul. And joy comes well in such a needy time :
What are they, I beseech your ladyship?

La. Cap. Well, well, thou hast a careful father, child ;
One who, to put thee from thy heaviness,
Hath sorted out a sudden day of joy,
That thou expect'st not, nor I look'd not for.

Jul. Madam, in happy time, what day is that?

La. Cap. Marry, my child, early next Thursday morn,
The gallant, young, and noble gentleman,
The County* Paris, at Saint Peter's Church,
Shall happily make thee there a joyful bride !

Jul. Now, by Saint Peter's Church, and Peter too,
He shall not make me there a joyful bride.
I wonder at this haste ; that I must wed
Ere he that should be husband comes to woo.
I pray you, tell my lord and father, madam,
I will not marry yet ; and, when I do, I swear,
It shall be Romeo, whom you know I hate,
Rather than Paris. These are news indeed !

La. Cap. Here comes your father ; tell him so yourself,
And see how he will take it at your hands.

Enter CAPULET *and* Nurse.

Cap. When the sun sets, the air doth drizzle dew ;
But for the sunset of my brother's son
It rains downright.
How now ! a conduit, girl? what, still in tears?
Evermore showering?

How now, wife!
Have you deliver'd to her our decree?

    La. Cap. Ay, sir; but she will none, she gives you thanks.
I would the fool were married to her grave!

    Cap. Soft! take me with you, take me with you, wife.
How! will she none? doth she not give us thanks?
Is she not proud? doth she not count her blest,
Unworthy as she is, that we have wrought
So worthy a gentleman to be her bridegroom?

    Jul. Not proud, you have, but thankful that you have:
Proud can I never be of what I hate;
But thankful even for hate that is meant love.

    Cap. How, how! how, how! chop-logic! What is this?
'Proud,' and 'I thank you,' and, 'I thank you not;'
And yet 'not proud:' mistress minion, you,
Thank me no thankings, nor proud me no prouds,
But fettle* your fine joints 'gainst Thursday next,
To go with Paris to Saint Peter's Church,
Or I will drag thee on a hurdle thither.

    Jul. Good father, I beseech you on my knees,
Hear me with patience but to speak a word.

    Cap. Hang thee, young baggage! disobedient wretch!
I tell thee what: get thee to church o' Thursday,
Or never after look me in the face:
Speak not, reply not, do not answer me;
My fingers itch. Wife, we scarce thought us blest
That God had lent us but this only child,
But now I see this one is one too much
And that we have a curse in having her:
Out on her, hilding!*

    Nurse.   God in heaven bless her!
You are to blame, my lord, to rate her so.

    Cap. And why, my lady wisdom? hold your tongue,
Good prudence; smatter with your gossips, go.

    Nurse. I speak no treason.

Cap.   Peace, you mumbling fool !
Utter your gravity o'er a gossip's bowl ;
For here we need it not.
  La. Cap.   You are too hot.
  Cap. It makes me mad :
Day, night, hour, tide, time, work, play,
Alone, in company, still my care hath been
To have her match'd : and having now provided
A gentleman of noble parentage,   ´
Of fair demesnes, youthful, and nobly train'd,
Stuff'd, as they say, with honourable parts,
Proportion'd as one's thought would wish a man ;
And then to have a wretched puling fool,
A whining mammet,* in her fortune's tender,
To answer 'I'll not wed ; I cannot love,
I am too young ; I pray you, pardon me.'
But, an you will not wed, I'll pardon you :
Graze where you will, you shall not house with me :
Look to't, think on't, I do not use to jest.
Thursday is near ; lay hand on heart, advise :
An you be mine, I'll give you to my friend ;
An you be not, hang, beg, starve, die in the streets,
For, by my soul, I'll ne'er acknowledge thee,
Nor what is mine shall never do thee good :
Trust to't, bethink you ; I'll not be forsworn.   [*Exit.*

  Jul. Is there no pity sitting in the clouds,
That sees into the bottom of my grief ?
O, sweet my mother, cast me not away !
Delay this marriage for a month, a week ;
Or, if you do not, make the bridal bed
In that dim monument where Tybalt lies.
  La. Cap. Talk not to me, for I'll not speak a word :
Do as thou wilt, for I have done with thee.   [*Exit.*

  Jul. O God !—O nurse, how shall this be prevented ?
What say'st thou ? hast thou not a word of joy ?
Some comfort, nurse.

Nurse.   Faith, here it is.
Romeo is banish'd, and all the world to nothing,
That he dares ne'er come back to challenge you ;
Or, if he do, it needs must be by stealth.
Then, since the case so stands as now it doth,
I think it best you married with the county.
O, he's a lovely gentleman ! Romeo's a dishclout to him.
  Jul. Speakest thou from thy heart ?
  Nurse. And from my soul too ; else beshrew them both.
  Jul. Amen !
  Nurse. What ?
  Jul. Well, thou hast comforted me marvellous much.
Go in, and tell my lady I am gone,
Having displeased my father, to Laurence' cell,
To make confession and to be absolved.
  Nurse. Marry, I will, and this is wisely done.   [*Exit.*
  Jul. Ancient damnation ! O most wicked fiend !
Is it more sin to wish me thus forsworn,
Or to dispraise my lord with that same tongue
Which she hath praised him with above compare
So many thousand times ? Go, counsellor ;
Thou and my bosom henceforth shall be twain.
I'll to the friar, to know his remedy :
If all else fail, myself have power to die.   [*Exit.*

ACT IV.

SCENE I. *Friar Laurence's cell.*

Enter FRIAR LAURENCE *and* PARIS.

  Fri. L. On Thursday, sir ? the time is very short.
  Par. My father Capulet will have it so ;
And I am nothing slow to slack his haste.
  Fri. L. You say you do not know the lady's mind :
Uneven is the course ; I like it not.

Par. Immoderately she weeps for Tybalt's death,
And therefore have I little talk'd of love,
For Venus smiles not in a house of tears.
Now, sir, her father counts it dangerous
That she doth give her sorrow so much sway,
And in his wisdom hastes our marriage,
To stop the inundation of her tears,
Which, too much minded by herself alone,
May be put from her by society :
Now do you know the reason of this haste.
  Fri. L. [*Aside*] I would I knew not why it should be slow'd.
Look, sir, here comes the lady towards my cell.

Enter JULIET.

  Par. Happily met, my lady and my wife !
  Jul. That may be, sir, when I may be a wife.
  Par. That may be must be, love, on Thursday next.
  Jul. What must be shall be.
  Fri. L.   That's a certain text.
  Par. Come you to make confession to this father ?
  Jul. To answer that, I should confess to you.
Are you at leisure, holy father, now ;
Or shall I come to you at evening mass ?*
  Fri. L. My leisure serves me, pensive daughter, now.
My lord, we must entreat the time alone.
  Par. God shield I should disturb devotion !
Juliet, on Thursday early will I rouse ye :
Till then, adieu !   [*Exit.*
  Jul. O, shut the door, and when thou hast done so,
Come weep with me ; past hope, past cure, past help !
  Fri. L. Ah, Juliet, I already know thy grief ;
It strains me past the compass of my wits :
I hear thou must, and nothing may prorogue it,
On Thursday next be married to this county.
  Jul. Tell me not, friar, that thou hear'st of this,   .

Unless thou tell me how I may prevent it :
If in thy wisdom thou canst give no help,
Do thou but call my resolution wise,
And with this knife I'll help it presently.
God join'd my heart and Romeo's, thou our hands ;
And ere this hand, by thee to Romeo's seal'd,
Shall be the label to another deed,
Or my true heart with treacherous revolt
Turn to another, this shall slay them both :
Therefore, out of thy long-experienced time,
Give me some present counsel ; or, behold,
'Twixt my extremes* and me this bloody knife
Shall play the umpire.

 Fri. L. Hold, daughter : I do spy a kind of hope,
Which craves as desperate an execution
As that is desperate which we would prevent.
If, rather than to marry County Paris,
Thou hast the strength of will to slay thyself,
Then is it likely thou wilt undertake
A thing like death to chide away this shame,
That copest with death himself to 'scape from it ;
And, if thou darest, I'll give thee remedy.

 Jul. O, bid me leap, rather than marry Paris,
From off the battlements of yonder tower ;
Or walk in thievish ways ; or bid me lurk
Where serpents are ; chain me with roaring bears ;
Or shut me nightly in a charnel-house,
O'er-cover'd quite with dead men's rattling bones,
With reeky shanks and yellow chapless skulls ;
Or bid me go into a new-made grave,
And hide me with a dead man in his shroud ;
Things that to hear them told, have made me tremble ;
And I will do it without fear or doubt,
To live an unstain'd wife to my sweet love.

 Fri. L. Hold, then ; go home, be merry, give consent

To marry Paris: Wednesday is to-morrow;
To-morrow night look that thou lie alone,
Let not thy nurse lie with thee in thy chamber:
Take thou this vial, being then in bed,
And this distilled liquor drink thou off:
When presently through all thy veins shall run
A cold and drowsy humour; for no pulse
Shall keep his native progress, but surcease:
No warmth, no breath, shall testify thou livest;
The roses in thy lips and cheeks shall fade
To paly ashes; thy eyes' windows fall,
Like death, when he shuts up the day of life;
Each part, deprived of supple government,
Shall, stiff and stark and cold, appear like death:
And in this borrow'd likeness of shrunk death
Thou shalt continue two and forty hours,
And then awake as from a pleasant sleep.
Now, when the bridegroom in the morning comes
To rouse thee from thy bed, there art thou dead:
Then, as the manner of our country is,
In thy best robes uncover'd on the bier
Thou shalt be borne to that same ancient vault
Where all the kindred of the Capulets lie.
In the mean time, against thou shalt awake,
Shall Romeo by my letters know our drift;
And hither shall he come: and he and I
Will watch thy waking, and that very night
Shall Romeo bear thee hence to Mantua.
And this shall free thee from this present shame,
If no inconstant toy* nor womanish fear
Abate thy valour in the acting it.

   Jul. Give me, give me! O, tell me not of fear!
Love give me strength! and strength shall help afford.
Farewell, dear father!   [*Exeunt.*

   4

SCENE II. *A room in Capulet's house.*

Enter CAPULET, LADY CAPULET, Nurse, PETER *and* SAMPSON.

Cap. So many guests invite as here are writ.   [*Exit Sampson.*
Sirrah, go hire me twenty cunning cooks.

Pet. You shall have none ill, sir, for I'll try if they can lick
their fingers.

Cap. How canst thou try them so ?

Pet. Marry, sir, 'tis an ill cook that cannot lick his own fingers : therefore he that cannot lick his fingers goes not with me.

Cap. Go, be gone.   [*Exit Peter.*
We shall be much unfurnish'd for this time.
What, is my daughter gone to Friar Laurence ?

Nurse. Ay, forsooth.

Cap. Well, he may chance to do some good on her :
A peevish self-will'd harlotry it is.

Nurse. See where she comes from shrift* with merry look.

Enter JULIET.

Cap. How now, my headstrong! where have you been gadding ?

Jul. Where I have learn'd me to repent the sin
Of disobedient opposition
To you and your behests, and am enjoin'd
By holy Laurence to fall prostrate here,
To beg your pardon : pardon, I beseech you !
Henceforward I am ever ruled by you.

Cap. Send for the county ; go tell him of this :
I'll have this knot knit up to-morrow morning.

Jul. I met the youthful lord at Laurence' cell,
And gave him what becomed* love I might,
Not stepping o'er the bounds of modesty.

Cap. Why, I am glad on't ; this is well : stand up :
This is as't should be.   Let me see the county ;
Ay, marry, go, I say, and fetch him hither,

Now, afore God, this reverend holy friar,
All our whole city is much bound to him.

  Jul. Nurse, will you go with me into my closet,
To help me sort such needful ornaments
As you think fit to furnish me to-morrow?

  La. Cap. No, not till Thursday; there is time enough.

  Cap. Go, nurse, go with her: we'll to church to-morrow.

                              [*Exeunt Juliet and Nurse.*

  La. Cap. We shall be short in our provision:
'Tis now near night.

  Cap.   Tush, I will stir about,
And all things shall be well, I warrant thee, wife:
Go thou to Juliet, help to deck up her;
I'll not to bed to-night; let me alone;
I'll play the housewife for this once. What, ho!
They are all forth: well, I will walk myself
To County Paris, to prepare him up
Against to-morrow: my heart is wondrous light,
Since this same wayward girl is so reclaim'd.   [*Exeunt.*

SCENE III.   *Juliet's chamber.*

Enter JULIET *and* Nurse.

  Jul. Ay, those attires are best: but, gentle nurse,
I pray thee, leave me to myself to-night;
For I have need of many orisons
To move the heavens to smile upon my state,
Which, well thou know'st, is cross and full of sin.

Enter LADY CAPULET.

  La. Cap. What, are you busy, ho? need you my help?

  Jul. No, madam; we have cull'd such necessaries
As are behoveful for our state to-morrow:
So please you, let me now be left alone,

And let the nurse this night sit up with you,
For I am sure you have your hands full all
In this so sudden business.

    La. Cap.   Good night :
Get thee to bed and rest, for thou hast need.

    Jul. Farewell !   [*Exeunt Lady Capulet and Nurse.*
                God knows when we shall meet again.
I have a faint cold fear thrills through my veins,
That almost freezes up the heat of life :
I'll call them back again to comfort me.
Nurse !—What should she do here ?
My dismal scene I needs must act alone.
Come, vial.
What if this mixture do not work at all ?
Shall I be married then to-morrow morning ?
No, no : this shall forbid it.   Lie thou there.
                    [*Laying down a dagger.*
What if it be a poison, which the friar
Subtly hath minister'd to have me dead,
Lest in this marriage he should be dishonour'd,
Because he married me before to Romeo ?
I fear it is : and yet, methinks, it should not,
For he hath still been tried a holy man.
How if, when I am laid into the tomb,
I wake before the time that Romeo
Come to redeem me ? there's a fearful point.
Shall I not then be stifled in the vault,
To whose foul mouth no healthsome air breathes in,
And there die strangled ere my Romeo comes ?
Or, if I live, is it not very like,
The horrible conceit of death and night,
Together with the terror of the place,
As in a vault, an ancient receptacle,
Where for this many hundred years the bones
Of all my buried ancestors are pack'd ;

Where bloody Tybalt, yet but green in earth,
Lies festering* in his shroud ; where, as they say,
At some hours in the night spirits resort ;
Alack, alack, is it not like that I
So early waking, what with loathsome smells
And shrieks like mandrakes'* torn out of the earth,
That living mortals hearing them run mad :
O, if I wake, shall I not be distraught,
Environed with all these hideous fears ?
And madly play with my forefathers' joints ?
And pluck the mangled Tybalt from his shroud ?
And, in this rage, with some great kinsman's bone,
As with a club, dash out my desperate brains ?
O, look ! methinks I see my cousin's ghost
Seeking out Romeo : stay, Tybalt, stay !
Romeo, I come ! this do I drink to thee !   [*The curtain falls.*

ACT V.

SCENE I. *Mantua. A street.*

Enter ROMEO.

Rom. If I may trust the flattering truth of sleep,
My dreams presage some joyful news at hand :
My bosom's lord sits lightly in his throne,
And all this day an unaccustom'd spirit
Lifts me above the ground with cheerful thoughts.
I dreamt my lady came and found me dead—
Strange dream, that gives a dead man leave to think ! —
And breathed such life with kisses in my lips
That I revived and was an emperor.
Ah me ! how sweet is love itself possess'd,
When but love's shadows are so rich in joy !

Enter BALTHASAR.

News from Verona !   How now, Balthasar !
Dost thou not bring me letters from the friar ?
How doth my lady ?   Is my father well ?
How fares my Juliet ? that I ask again ;
For nothing can be ill, if she be well.

Bal. Then she is well, and nothing can be ill :
Her body sleeps in Capels' monument,
And her immortal part with angels lives.
I saw her laid low in her kindred's vault,
And presently took post to tell it you :
O, pardon me for bringing these ill news,
Since you did leave it for my office, sir.

Rom. Is it e'en so ? then I defy you, stars !
Thou know'st my lodging : get me ink and paper,
And hire post-horses ; I will hence to-night.

Bal. I do beseech you, sir, have patience :
Your looks are pale and wild, and do import
Some misadventure.

Rom.   Tush, thou art deceived :
Leave me, and do the thing I bid thee do.
Hast thou no letters to me from the friar ?

Bal. No, my good lord.

Rom.   No matter : get thee gone,
And hire those horses ; I'll be with thee straight. [*Exit Balthasar.*
Well, Juliet, I will lie with thee to-night.
Let's see for means :—O mischief, thou art swift
To enter in the thoughts of desperate men !
I do remember an apothecary,
And hereabouts a' dwells, which late I noted
In tatter'd weeds, with overwhelming brows,
Culling of simples ; meagre were his looks ;
Sharp misery had worn him to the bones :
And in his needy shop a tortoise hung,
An alligator stuff'd and other skins

Or ill-shaped fishes; and about his shelves
A beggarly account of empty boxes,
Green earthen pots, bladders, and musty seeds,
Remnants of packthread and old cakes of roses,
Were thinly scatter'd, to make up a show.
Noting this penury, to myself I said,
An if a man did need a poison now,
Whose sale is present death in Mantua,
Here lives a caitiff wretch would sell it him.
O, this same thought did but forerun my need,
And this same needy man must sell it me.
As I remember, this should be the house:
Being holiday, the beggar's shop is shut.
What ho! apothecary!

Enter Apothecary.

Ap.   Who calls so loud?
Rom. Come hither, man. I see that thou art poor;
Hold, there is forty ducats: let me have
A dram of poison; such soon-speeding gear
As will disperse itself through all the veins,
That the life-weary taker may fall dead.
Ap. Such mortal drugs I have; but Mantua's law
Is death to any he that utters them.
Rom. Art thou so bare and full of wretchedness,
And fear'st to die? famine is in thy cheeks,
Need and oppression starveth in thy eyes,
Contempt and beggary hangs upon thy back,
The world is not thy friend, nor the world's law:
The world affords no law to make thee rich;
Then be not poor, but break it, and take this.
Ap. My poverty, but not my will, consents.
Rom. I pray thy poverty and not thy will.
Ap. Put this in any liquid thing you will,
And drink it off; and, if you had the strength

Of twenty men, it would dispatch you straight.

   Rom. There is thy gold, worse poison to men's souls,
Doing more murder in this loathsome world,
Than these poor compounds that thou mayst not sell :
I sell thee poison, thou hast sold me none.
Farewell : buy food, and get thyself in flesh.   [*Exit Apothecary.*
Come, cordial and not poison, go with me
To Juliet's grave, for there must I use thee.   [*Exit.*

SCENE II. *Friar Laurence's cell.*

Enter FRIAR JOHN.

   Fri. J. Holy Franciscan friar ! brother, ho ! ·

Enter FRIAR LAURENCE.

   Fri. L. This same should be the voice of Friar John.
Welcome from Mantua : what says Romeo ?
Or, if his mind be writ, give me his letter.

   Fri. J. Going to find a bare-foot brother out,
One of our order, to associate me,[1]
Here in this city visiting the sick,
And finding him, the searchers of the town,
Suspecting that we both were in a house
Where the infectious pestilence did reign,
Seal'd up the doors and would not let us forth ;
So that my speed to Mantua there was stay'd.

   Fri. L. Who bare my letter then to Romeo ?

   Fri. J. I could not send it,—here it is again,—
Nor get a messenger to bring it thee,
So fearful were they of infection.

   Fri. L. Unhappy fortune ! by my brotherhood,
The letter was not nice,* but full of charge
Of dear import, and the neglecting it

Each friar had always a companion assigned him by the superior, when he asked
leave to go out.

May do much danger.   Friar John, go hence ;
Get me an iron crow and bring it straight
Unto my cell.
   Fri. J. Brother, I'll go and bring it thee.   [*Exit.*
   Fri. L. Now must I to the monument alone ;
Within this three hours will fair Juliet wake :
She will beshrew me much that Romeo
Hath had no notice of these accidents ;
But I will write again to Mantua,
And keep her at my cell till Romeo come :
Poor living corse, closed in a dead man's tomb !   [*Exit*

SCENE III.   *A churchyard; in it a monument belonging to the*
Capulets.

Enter PARIS *and his* Page, *bearing flowers and a torch.*

   Par. Give me thy torch, boy : hence, and stand aloof :
Yet put it out, for I would not be seen.
Under yond yew-trees lay thee all along,
Holding thine ear close to the hollow ground ;
So shall no foot upon the churchyard tread,
Being loose, unfirm, with digging up of graves,
But thou shalt hear it : whistle then to me,
As signal that thou hear'st something approach.
Give me those flowers.   Do as I bid thee, go.
   Page. [*Aside*] I am almost afraid to stand alone
Here in the churchyard ; yet I will adventure.   [*Retires.*
   Par. Sweet flower, with flowers thy bridal bed I strew,—
   O woe ! thy canopy is dust and stones ;—
Which with sweet water nightly I will dew,
   Or, wanting that, with tears distill'd by moans :
The obsequies that I for thee will keep
Nightly shall be to strew, thy grave and weep.
                                   [*The Page whistles.*
   4*

The boy gives warning something doth approach.
What cursed foot wanders this way to-night,
To cross my obsequies and true love's rite ?
What, with a torch !   Muffle me, night, awhile.   *[Retires.*

Enter ROMEO *and* BALTHASAR, *with a torch, wrenching iron, &c.*

   Rom. Give me the wrenching iron.
Hold, take this letter; early in the morning
See thou deliver it to my lord and father.
Set down the light : upon thy life, I charge thee,
Whate'er thou hear'st or seest, stand all aloof,
And do not interrupt me in my course.
Why I descend into this bed of death
Is partly to behold my lady's face,
But chiefly to take thence from her dead finger
A precious ring, a ring that I must use
In dear employment : therefore hence, be gone :
But if thou, jealous, dost return to pry
In what I farther shall intend to do,
By heaven, I will tear thee joint by joint
And strew this hungry churchyard with thy limbs :
The time and my intents are savage-wild,
More fierce and more inexorable far
Than empty tigers or the roaring sea.
   Bal. I will be gone, sir, and not trouble you.
   Rom. So shalt thou show me friendship.   Take thou that :
Live, and be prosperous : and farewell, good fellow.
   Bal. [*Aside*] For all this same, I'll hide me hereabout :
His looks I fear, and his intents I doubt.   *[Retires.*
   Rom. Thou detestable maw, thou womb of death,
Gorged with the dearest morsel of the earth,
Thus I enforce thy rotten jaws to open,
And in despite I'll cram thee with more food.   *[Opens the tomb.*
   Par. This is that banish'd haughty Montague
That murder'd my love's cousin, with which grief,

It is supposed,the fair creature died,
And here is come to do some villanous shame
To the dead bodies : I will apprehend him. [*Comes forward.*
Stop thy unhallow'd toil, vile Montague !
Can vengeance be pursued further than death ?
Condemned villain, I do apprehend thee :
Obey, and go with me ; for thou must die.

 Rom. I must indeed, and therefore came I hither.
Good gentle youth, tempt not a desperate man ;
Fly hence and leave me : think upon these gone ;
Let them affright thee. I beseech thee, youth,
Put not another sin upon my head,
By urging me to fury : O, be gone !
By heaven, I love thee better than myself,
For I come hither arm'd against myself :
Stay not, be gone : live, and hereafter say,
A madman's mercy bid thee run away.

 Par. I do defy thy conjurations
And apprehend thee for a felon here.

 Rom. Wilt thou provoke me ? then have at thee, boy !
           [*They fight.*

 Page. O Lord, they fight ! I will go call the watch. [*Exit.*

 Par. O, I am slain ! [*Falls.*] If thou be merciful,
Open the tomb, lay me with Juliet. [*Dies.*

 Rom. In faith, I will. Let me peruse this face :
Mercutio's kinsman, noble County Paris !
What said my man, when my betossed soul
Did not attend him as we rode ? I think
He told me Paris should have married Juliet :
Said he not so ? or did I dream it so ?
Or am I mad, hearing him talk of Juliet,
To think it was so ? O, give me thy hand,
One writ with me in sour misfortune's book !
I'll bury thee in a triumphant grave ;
For here lies Juliet—O my love ! my wife !

Death, that hath suck'd the honey of thy breath,
Hath had no power yet upon thy beauty:
Thou art not conquer'd; beauty's ensign yet
Is crimson in thy lips and in thy cheeks,
And death's pale flag is not advanced there.
Tybalt, liest thou there in thy bloody sheet?
O, what more favour can I do thee
Than with that hand that cut thy youth in twain
To sunder his that was thine enemy?
Forgive me, cousin! Ah, dear Juliet,
Why art thou yet so fair? shall I believe
That unsubstantial death is amorous,
And that the lean abhorred monster keeps
Thee here in dark to be his paramour?
For fear of that, I still will stay with thee,
And never from this palace of dim night
Depart again: here, here will I remain
With worms that are thy chamber-maids; O, here
Will I set up my everlasting rest,
And shake the yoke of inauspicious stars   •
From this world-wearied flesh.   Eyes, look your last!
Arms, take your last embrace! and, lips, O you
The doors of breath, seal with a righteous kiss
A dateless bargain to engrossing death!
Come, bitter conduct,* come, unsavoury guide!
Thou desperate pilot, now at once run on
The dashing rocks thy sea-sick weary bark.
Here's to my love! [*Drinks.*]   O true apothecary!
Thy drugs are quick.   Thus with a kiss I die.   [*Dies.*

Enter, at the other end of the churchyard, FRIAR LAURENCE, *with a
lantern, crow, and spade.*

Fri. L. Saint Francis be my speed! how oft to-night
Have my old feet stumbled at graves!   [*Advances.*
Alack, alack, what blood is this, which stains

The stony entrance of this sepulchre?
Romeo! O, pale! Who else? what, Paris, too?
And steep'd in blood? Ah, what an unkind hour
Is guilty of this lamentable chance!
The lady stirs.   [*Juliet wakes.*

   Jul. O comfortable friar! where is my lord?
I do remember well where I should be,
And there I am: where is my Romeo?   [*Noise within.*

   Fri. L. I hear some noise. Lady, come from that nest
Of death, contagion and unnatural sleep:
A greater power than we can contradict
Hath thwarted our intents: come, come away:
Thy husband in thy bosom there lies dead;
And Paris too: come, I'll dispose of thee
Among a sisterhood of holy nuns: [*Noise within increases.*
Stay not to question, for the watch is coming;
Come, go, good Juliet; I dare no longer stay.

   Jul. Go, get thee hence, for I will not away.
                      [*Exit Friar Laurence.*

What's here?
Poison, I see, hath been his timeless end:
O churl! drunk all, and left no friendly drop
To help me after? I will kiss thy lips;
Haply some poison yet doth hang on them,
To make me die with a restorative.   [*Kisses him.*

   Watch. [*Within*] Lead, boy: which way?
   Jul. Yea, noise? then I'll be brief. O happy dagger!
               [*Snatching Romeo's dagger.*
This is thy sheath; [*Stabs herself*] there rust, and let me die.
           [*Falls on Romeo's body and dies*

Enter the Watch *and* Others.

               [*The curtain falls.*

GLOSSARY.

Alla stoccata, the Italian term of art for the thrust with a rapier.

Atomy, an atom.

Becomed, becoming.

Carry coals, to put up with insults.

Catling, a lute-string.

Cheveril, kid leather.

Conceit, imagination.

Conduct, leader, conductor.

Consort, an old term for a set or company of musicians.

Contrary, to oppose.

Countervail, to counterpoise, outweigh.

County, count, earl.

Court-cupboard, sideboard.

Cousin, used in addressing kinsmen of different degrees.

Crow-keeper, one who scares crows.

Desperate, determined, bold.

Dislike, displease.

Division, a phrase or passage in a melody.

Envious, malicious.

Evening-mass, vespers.

Extremes, extremities.

Fantastic, a fantastical person.

Fester, to corrupt.

Fettle, to make ready.

Flecked, spotted, streaked.

Flirt-gill, a light woman.

Good-den, good-evening, contracted from 'good-even.'

Hall, an open space to dance in.

Hay, a term in fencing, equivalent to the Latin *habet* (he has it) at the gladiatorial shows.

Hilding, a base woman, a low wretch.

Humourous, fitful, whimsical.

Hunts-up, a holla used in hunting when the game was on foot.

Indite, to invite.

Inherit, to possess.

Lenten, that which may be eaten in Lent.

Mammet, a doll.

Mandrake, a plant of soporiferous quality, supposed to resemble a man.

Marchpane, a kind of sweet biscuit.

Measure, a stately dance.

Mew, a hawk's cage.

Mistempered, angry.

Nice, trivial.

Palmer, one who bears a palm-branch, in token of having made a pilgrimage to Palestine.

Part, 'with that part'—Act II., Scene 3; used in the sense of *with its odor*.

Passado, the name of a thrust in fencing.

Peer, to peep out.

Pilcher, a scabbard.

Pin, the center of a target.

Poor John, a term applied to salted hake; a kind of fish not much esteemed.

Prick-song, music sung in parts by note.

Princox, a coxcomb.

Procure, to bring.

Prorogue, to defer.

Punto reverso, the name of a thrust in fencing.

Quote, to note.

Rebeck, a three-stringed violin.

Respective, thoughtful, considerate.

Rood, the crucifix.

Ropery, roguery.

Rush, to push.

Said, 'well said,'—Act I., Scene 5; used in the sense of *well done*.

Scant, scarcely.

Scathe, to injure.

Shrift, confession.

Skains-mates, scapegraces.

Slip, a piece of base money.

Smoothe, to flatter, speak fair.

Sped, settled, done for.

Strange, coy, reserved.

Suit, a place in court.

Swashing, dashing, smashing.

Sweeting, the name of an apple.

Tassel-gentle, an elegant and highly-trained hawk.

Teen, sorrow.

Towards, nearly ready

Toy, freak, caprice.

Validity, worth, value.

The Works of Charles Dickens.

GLOBE EDITION.

The Cheapest Legible Edition ever Published.

Printed in large type, on fine paper, and containing all the illustrations of Darley and Gilbert, complete in 13 vols., 12mo.

1. Nicholas Nickleby.	7. David Copperfield.
2. Old Curiosity Shop, and Part I. Sketches.	8. Tale of Two Cities, and Hard Times.
	9. Bleak House.
3. Barnaby Rudge, and Part II. Sketches.	10. Little Dorrit.
	11. Christmas Stories, American Notes, and Pictures from Italy.
4. Martin Chuzzlewit.	
5. Dombey and Son.	12. Our Mutual Friend.
6. Oliver Twist, and Great Expectations.	13. Pickwick Papers.

Price, in cloth, per volume ....$ 1 50

The set, green crape cloth 19 50

" " half calf, extra.....:.. 39 00

RIVERSIDE EDITION.

Printed on fine paper, and containing all the illustrations that have appeared in the English edition, by CRUIKSHANK, PHIZ, SEYMOUR, JOHN LEACH, D. MACLISE, MARCUS STONE, and others, elegantly engraved on steel, to which are added the unsurpassed designs of F. O. C. DARLEY and JOHN GILBERT, now used in the Household Edition, making this at once the most complete and elegant edition ever offered to the public in America or England. Complete in twenty-six volumes, crown 8vo.

Oliver Twist............................1 vol.	Tale of Two Cities..................1 vol.
Nicholas Nickleby....................2 vols.	Bleak House.............. ....2 vols.
Martin Chuzzlewit..................2 vols.	Hard Times..........................1 vol.
Christmas Stories.....................1 vol.	Little Dorrit............. ....2 vols.
Old Curiosity Shop, and Part I. Sketches... ....2 vols.	American Notes and Pictures from Italy........... ....1 vol.
Barnaby Rudge, and Part II. Sketches ....2 vols.	Great Expectations..................1 vol.
	Our Mutual Friend..................2 vols.
Dombey and Son...,.................2 vols.	Pickwick Papers.....................2 vols
David Copperfield....................2 vols.	

Price, in cloth, $2.50 per volume. In half calf, extra, $4.00.

HOUSEHOLD EDITION.

Printed on toned paper, and illustrated from drawings by F. O. C. Darley and John Gilbert. Complete in fifty-three volumes.

Prices.—Green vellum cloth, cut or uncut, per volume.................$ 1 25

The set, crape cloth, fifty-three volumes.................................. 66 25

The set, half calf, gilt, or half morocco.....................................132 50

HURD AND HOUGHTON, Publishers,

459 BROOME STREET, NEW YORK.

www.ingramcontent.com/pod-product-compliance
Lightning Source LLC
Chambersburg PA
CBHW022013050726
47499CB00007BA/2560